Redemption

The Guardian Angel Series
Book 4

S. Hamil
Sharon Hamilton

S. Hamil's Book List

PARANORMALS

GOLDEN VAMPIRES OF TUSCANY SERIES
Honeymoon Bite Book 1
Mortal Bite Book 2
Christmas Bite Book 3
Midnight Bite Book 4

THE GUARDIANS
Heavenly Lover Book 1
Underworld Lover Book 2
Underworld Queen Book 3
Redemption Book 4

FALL FROM GRACE SERIES
Gideon: Heavenly Fall

SEAL BROTHERHOOD BOOKS

SEAL BROTHERHOOD SERIES
Accidental SEAL Book 1
Fallen SEAL Legacy Book 2
SEAL Under Covers Book 3
SEAL The Deal Book 4
Cruisin' For A SEAL Book 5
SEAL My Destiny Book 6
SEAL of My Heart Book 7

Fredo's Dream Book 8

SEAL My Love Book 9

SEAL Encounter Prequel to Book 1

SEAL Endeavor Prequel to Book 2

Ultimate SEAL Collection Vol. 1 Books 1-4 /2 Prequels

Ultimate SEAL Collection Vol. 2 Books 5-7

BAD BOYS OF SEAL TEAM 3 SERIES

SEAL's Promise Book 1

SEAL My Home Book 2

SEAL's Code Book 3

Big Bad Boys Bundle Books 1-3

BAND OF BACHELORS SERIES

Lucas Book 1

Alex Book 2

Jake Book 3

Jake 2 Book 4

Big Band of Bachelors Bundle

BONE FROG BROTHERHOOD SERIES

New Year's SEAL Dream Book 1

SEALed At The Altar Book 2

SEALed Forever Book 3

SEAL's Rescue Book 4

SEALed Protection Book 5

SUNSET SEALS SERIES

SEALed at Sunset

Second Chance SEAL

Treasure Island SEAL

Escape to Sunset

SILVER SEALS SERIES

SEAL Love's Legacy

SLEEPER SEALS SERIES

Bachelor SEAL

STAND ALONE BOOKS & SERIES

SEAL's Goal: The Beautiful Game

Nashville SEAL: Jameson

True Blue SEALS Zak

Paradise: In Search of Love

Love Me Tender, Love You Hard

NOVELLAS

SEAL You In My Dreams Magnolias and Moonshine

SEAL Of Time Trident Legacy

All of S. Hamil's books are available on Audible, narrated by the talented J.D. Hart.

About The Guardians Series

Heaven was created by design. The Underworld was created by accident.

The Guardians series is a unique twist on Guardian Angels in the stunning world building of Sharon's imagination. We are given a saga of events, from Claire's falling in love with her human charge, Daniel, to the eventual conversion of the dark angel Joshua to hero in Books 2 and again in Book 4. We have Audray's story: the first-ever woman Director of the Underworld. A cast of creative and mind-blowing characters accompany these lush and rich stories of pure Good vs. Evil, in its primal form, all with Happily Ever Afters!

About the Book

Former Dark Angel Joshua Brandon has skirted a forever un-death in the Underworld until his heart yanks him from his life of debauchery and back into the Human World. He has accepted a very stealth assignment from the man upstairs to perhaps obtain those white wings he's never wanted until now.

But it will require him turning back to the dark side. And just after his promise is made, the only woman he's ever loved comes back into his life. She is in desperate need of saving. But as a Dark Angel, the only thing he can do is claim her soul for his own in the Underworld.

Will he have to throw away any hope of redemption, in order to save her?

Book 4 in this popular series about Guardian Angels, Dark Angels, the healing power of love, and good vs. evil. Although, evil can be more fun!

Remember, in this world: Heaven is created by design. The Underworld is created by accident.

Dedication

This is a special book to me. In 2008 our house burned down. A lifetime of possessions were lost, and oddly, some survived. Thankfully, no one was injured. The fire was as indiscriminate as fate is. What happened as a horrific event turned into a miracle.

While we were recovering and deciding what to do with the house, haggling with the insurance and our mortgage lender (being taken over by the Feds in another cruel twist of fate), a new vision began to emerge. It took several years to finish this project, but along the way, I was visited by what I can only say were Guardian Angels, who held my hand and helped me deal with all the decisions and life-changing things going on around me.

I began to have dreams of these angels. I wondered what their personalities were like. The image of Claire, the scrappy, highly successful and bright-spirited angel came to mind. Just like I was recovering from the depths of despair, I had Claire ministering to people who had found themselves devoid of the tools to go on. She brought my hero, Daniel, the strength to realize the beauty of his own life, just as she gave something to me. Something priceless.

I became a writer.

In thinking about Claire and her needs, I wondered if she could fall in love. What would that love look like? Is there such a thing as angelic love? Guardian Angel love? What would that feel like, and how would she be able to do this?

And so my story was born. So was the career of a new writer, from a place hidden by "stuff" I no longer needed, uncovered and purged by a fire in the middle of a February night.

I was lucky to meet a group of amazing writers through three RWA chapters I joined: San Francisco RWA, Silicon Valley RWA and Black Diamonds RWA (sadly this chapter has closed). I also joined Redwood Writers and California Writers Clubs. I joined a multi-genre critique group called the Tuesday Group (which now meets on Thursdays). I contested this manuscript and rewrote it more than 57 times. I finaled in contests and took dozens of classes, searched for an agent, a publisher and a following.

It all worked. I was given not always what I asked for, but what I needed most.

This is more than a story. It is the work of my heart, once damaged and full of pain, rehealed by stories of true love and a happily ever after.

Because that's where I really live.

Enjoy!

Chapter 1

JOSHUA BRANDON SAT on the cold, concrete bench at the San Francisco Palace of Fine Arts. He watched the ducks and pigeons play in the late morning coolness that would not end. He always found things colder these days, especially San Francisco, this cloudless day. There was just enough breeze to keep him from getting comfortable.

Perhaps if I'd relocated to some place warmer, some place like Florida or even Southern California, maybe then my body would warm.

But even his soul brooded these days.

He was waiting for the big man himself to show up, and, as usual, Father was late. Joshua thought it odd that the Supreme Being of all things would not be able to maintain a schedule.

"Perfection is measured in many different ways," boomed the familiar husky baritone of the man from the cloud kingdom, as Joshua had lately been calling him.

The voice rattled his insides, not from fear, but as a grim reminder Father could still read his thoughts. When Joshua had been a dark angel with enormous, shiny black wings, that skill was lost on Father. Alas, these past nearly ten years, Joshua had adopted the human form he'd been granted by way of a pardon. He always knew that pardon came with not white wings, but strings.

Joshua nodded, and waited for the man in the white suit to take his place beside him on the bench. He could feel the body heat, the absence of scent, and the deafening silence that worked like a vacuum around the man as he effortlessly sat down and pondered on the duckpond.

"I hear stories that you are well and have been tending your little flock of friends," the big man said.

"Such as they are," Joshua retorted. He sometimes felt like a bandleader for a bunch of randy teenagers who couldn't carry a tune to save their souls.

"That's funny," Father said. He must have looked puzzled because Father added, "The randy teenagers who couldn't carry a tune to save their souls."

"Ah, yes." Joshua gazed upon the Creator himself. In profile, his pale skin hadn't aged, of course, even with all the burdens of his high office. For who helps the Creator of all things? He wondered if the man ever got lonely. His blue eyes were still the color of the sky, except when he got angry. "You've experienced this, then? You sometimes feel like a bandleader to a world continually playing off key?" Joshua asked.

Father smiled, leaned forward and extended his fingers out for a wayward duckling who chanced to waddle up to them both. He let the duckling stand in the palm of his hand and do a pirouette as if he was on show. He examined his handiwork of this fuzzy yellow creature and then set him down to return to the flock of nonplussed fowl gliding through the clear water.

Joshua noted the man's fondness for things with feathers.

"The miracle of creation hinges on the fact that life is a tapestry of harmony and disharmony, intention and chaos, free will and compulsion." He winked and added, "Yes, feathers and fangs. It's the DNA of everything. There cannot be life without variety, and that means not everyone plays the same note, or even wants to be in a band, and yet they all are." The old man turned to face him. "Aren't they?"

In Father's blue orbs, Joshua saw the movies containing histories of peoples and worlds he had yet to experience. He saw the flames, the armies, the fields of corn and wheat, the rivers and angry oceans both in the future and long past. He wondered what it was like inside the man's brain, for surely, he had one.

"I do," Father answered.

Joshua tore himself away just in case he was being shown something he would not like to see. Again, he waited.

"I summoned you today because I wanted to continue the conversation we had several eons ago when I asked you to help me with something."

"And I promised I would."

"You did, Son."

"But you gave me until the end of my lifetime. So, does this mean you know something I don't?" Josh's blood pressure spiked as his stomach rumbled.

"You already know the answer to that Joshua, my friend. But, if I'd wanted a date certain, I would have commanded it. I was hoping that your path here in the human world would be a little clearer cut. Purposeful. More anchored."

Josh's three centuries of existence were mostly as a dark angel. He had more excesses than he could remember. One of the problems he'd faced being human was what he missed.

Excitement.

He'd remained close with the former guardian, Claire and her little family. He helped former dark angels Audray and Jonas and their little one, as well as others of their flock, but they weren't really his kind of people. He could still taste the RedX that used to course through his veins, smell the smoky sins of the flesh laced with some of the finest spirits the Underworld could create. He'd sampled everything on the menu at Helena's brothel, even the fallen angels who lived there to service whatever creature that came prowling through her parlor. He had to admit that the sex was bolder and more enticing. The variety mindblowing. Excess taken for the pure joy of having excesses outweighed any kind of common sense or decency.

He wasn't afraid to let his thoughts wander so that Father could grasp what he was struggling with. Even if he tried, it was impossible not to be totally honest with the man. That's just the way it worked.

Vanilla.

He wasn't wrestling with some dark demon. He was grappling with vanilla. It's what sent Melanie away. And after that happened, Josh had trouble hiding the fact that his human life had started on a downward slide.

"It always looks better than it is," Father whispered.

"I'm ashamed to say that now, years later, after being given my chance at being human, I miss who I used to be. I just know too much," Josh said, studying the patterns on the lake all the ducks were making. "I mean, if you decided to become a duckling for a day, you would still know about the dogs, cats and coyotes out there lurking in the bushes, trying to grasp your tail fuzz."

Father laughed out loud at that vision. He was nearly crying. "Logic tells you, my son, that—if you were to go back—you'd soon discover what you'd thrown away. It's a dangerous and slippery slope. Yet, I must ask this of you now."

A lightning rod shot through Joshua. He was unaccustomed to being so surprised.

"Go back?"

"You made a promise you may not be able to keep, but I'm going to remind you of it. I'm sure Claire told you about the graveyard in Heaven."

Joshua shivered. "She did." It was an image he couldn't get out of his head. Headstones sitting in a grassy field among the clouds in Heaven, inscribed with the names of angels who had once been guardians. And all of these were of his doing. They'd shown them to Claire before she went down on her mission to protect Daniel. Claire won. It had been Joshua who had failed for the first time.

"I want you to bring them home. It's time. You know I can't go there."

He'd been preoccupied with the failure image and this shocked him back to present time. "But you *made* all the rules. Why don't you just *change* them?"

"It doesn't work that way. I had thought that perhaps they'd redeem themselves. Ask for forgiveness, repent and ask to be returned home. Alas, I miscalculated."

The conversation was giving Josh a headache.

"You?"

"It was an experiment." Father leaned back on the bench, resting his hands to the sides.

"We've had the discussion about free will before, Joshua. I won't change this feature. Everything is an experiment, for how else could creation, well, *create*?"

It was Josh's time to belly laugh. He didn't have to be as careful with Father as he would another acquaintance. Father knew everything inside his head. "That's rather like talking and then interrupting yourself."

The old man didn't take the bait. With a straight face, he replied, "Oh, I would never do that." Father flicked away something that had landed on his white jacket, crossed his legs, and stared back at the ducks.

"You're messing with me," Josh sputtered.

Father slowly angled his head and then twisted to

face him. "All the time. It is one of my favorite pas-times." Then he smiled. "I allow the characters to color in their own detail. Some struggle with their decisions. Others get it right the first time and need no further adjustment. Most humans grow through their trial and error." He kissed his fingertips. "The magic of life, Joshua. Nothing is sweeter. Lessons learned. Wisdom gained. Character formed."

The former dark angel thought it was possible the old man was becoming senile.

Father's shaking finger told him to be careful with those thoughts.

"It's like childbirth. The struggle helps the child survive, to thrive. Choice creates responsibility." He tapped Joshua on the shoulder. "Even for you, my son."

Joshua had always thought of himself as taking the easy way out. He didn't like to stew and worry. It was a useless enterprise. But not being able to enjoy things he used to love as a dark angel had left him wounded inside. "I don't have much of a conscience. How else would I have been so successful all those hundreds of years? And it was so satisfying claiming all those guardian souls. Those angelic creatures are the top of the food chain. You did well with them. But you created them much too naive. Surely you realize this."

Father's body heat rose. Joshua wondered if he'd gone too far.

"Which is why you're given the task now. You needed a cattle prod, my son. So, consider this your morning wake-up call. You have a feat of great importance to fulfill. You stole those angelic souls from me. Now I want them back. How you do it, how you accomplish this is not of my concern. I just want them returned, all those who will come willingly. No force is to be used."

Joshua felt the old man's eyes on him again. He was waiting for the light bulb to go on inside his head.

As if he needed to prod him one more time, Father added, "I've waited long enough. They've had their fun. Time for them to come home to a life they were created for. And I believe you are the only one who can make this happen."

Father stood, then began walking toward the lake's edge to examine the baby ducklings swimming by in a line, not paying him any attention at all.

The former dark angel felt sick to his stomach as the revelation descended upon him. "You mean, you want me to go *back* to the Underworld? To give up my human life?"

Father abruptly whirled around, crossed his arms, and smiled. "Exactly!" He scratched his chin, squinting one eye as he did so. "Tell me, Joshua Brandon, is this the life you thought it would be? Would you have chosen this for yourself if it was your decision?"

"I asked for it, Father."

"That's a different answer to a different question, Joshua. Today, right now, would this be the life you would choose this minute?"

The former dark angel scanned the centuries of his former life and the brief human existence he had now. Something was missing. The black hole that was left behind when Melanie left could never be repaired. He'd failed with her because he didn't have any of his magical powers to use. Everything about being alive lacked luster. Even sex was boring. He'd let her drift away through lack of attention. He'd been distracted with the aches in his human body, how flaccid his bodily functions were. Even eating repulsed him these days. Consuming too much alcohol wasn't fun, because the next day he felt like shit. There weren't any days like that in the Underworld or in the mortal realm as a dark angel. Formerly he could fly. He could love with abandon, and he could vaporize anybody who got in his way.

He'd been an energy-consuming, self-indulgent machine, and as a common man, he even irked himself with his own problems.

He'd once dangled the possibility of eternal life to Audray just before he turned her. Lured her with unlimited powers and a body in its most perfect state forever. Her groveling was over, he told her. She took the bait.

Only one thing that could be possibly be worth turning back to the dark side for. The task of retrieving Father's little flock of former guardians wasn't it. Did he dare ask this?

"She was gullible, Joshua. She's on her way to the Underworld to find you because that's what she'd been told. She's only just arriving, but I warn you, once she gets there, she'll not last long."

Chapter 2

MELANIE WORTHINGTON FOLLOWED behind the slender newspaper reporter who had sponsored her trip. He'd written an article about Joshua Brandon, the legendary art collector and agent to aging rock star painters which piqued her interest. Joshua had been her lover once. His dark angel wings had been clipped off by the man in the clouds, so they could spend the rest of their lives together and live in her human world.

Except that hadn't worked out.

The ache of missing him had not subsided. She suspected he'd lost interest in her and had been told of his infidelities by several other women who then disappeared after delivering their damning messages. Perhaps she'd misjudged him. He'd claimed his innocence. Maybe he'd been right all along.

Melanie knew he hadn't been perfect when she met him. Of course, that also was because he was a dark angel then. Just thinking about his fingers on her burning flesh made her blood warm, her heart beat wildly, and her panties moisten. Still today. The sensations were just as strong as in those heady days when he introduced her to his world of sex, flying through the night sky, and all the interesting places and people he knew about. And she'd nearly sacrificed herself to save him, too.

I could have spent eternity as a Guardian.

Father had told her so. Guardians were all about sacrifice. Dark angels were about indulgence and living forever in a peak state.

But the miracle that had been bestowed upon them didn't last. He'd broken her heart. The cavern of her soul still left her wanting what she had thrown away even though he no longer had those dark angel powers.

So, Naveen Broadchurch, the creepy reporter she contacted, brought her to this junction. To this place, so dangerously close to where he told her Joshua now lived.

"You are sure the visitors' passes will be accepted, Naveen?"

"My dear, it's all been arranged. You'll soon see for yourself."

He always looked so attentive as he bowed his head and gave that flat-lipped smile that extended nearly to his ears. His handsome face was hard to tear her focus from. His bright red lips hinted he might wear lip stain, and in shadow, they nearly glowed. His eyes certainly did, as if lit from within. Although human, Naveen had an aura of an actor playing the part of a dark vampire lord who couldn't get enough of his own character. She wondered if he slept in pajamas or animal skin. He had a keen sense of smell, even guessing the exact flowery recipe of her custom-made perfume scent.

But she knew it was all an act. She didn't really believe he was anything other than another man trying to get into her pants by currying favor with her. Well, she'd take the favor but had no intention of granting him his wish.

Just then, he turned and gave her a bone-chilling grin. "We're nearly there. Excited?" he asked as his eyes sparkled, giving her a sultry wink. He opened the warehouse door. Darkness consumed them both. It was so black and so dark, she felt like she'd stepped inside a huge black cloud of smoke.

"Be careful. I've taken you the back way, so we don't have any official interference," he whispered. "To avoid unnecessary risks or sacrifice."

Risks or sacrifice, sure thing, Naveen. I should hope so!

Melanie didn't let go of his hand because she couldn't see a thing. Water dripped somewhere. A cool wind swung through the warehouse with a gentle moan. The echoes of their steps on the wet concrete floor occasionally traveled over pieces of paper and wood scattered about. But a huge question was beginning to loom in the darkness. Her fingers felt stiff and constricted in Naveen's large hand, and the more she reacted to his touch, the tighter he hung on.

"You don't want to get lost, dear. As long as I'm with you, there is no danger, but, sorry to say, there is no light just yet. Soon, though. We'll be in full light soon. And there will be heat."

"Why didn't you bring a flashlight?"

She felt the whirl in the air as he turned to face her again. "My apologies, dear Melanie. I simply forgot."

Something was off about his response.

"But Naveen, I—I thought that's why we got the passes. Took the blood testing. I thought we avoided all this. Why do we have to go the back way?"

He abruptly stopped. A sliver of light was coming from somewhere and she could only barely see him. There was no mistaking the heat of his liver-colored lips as he whispered into her left ear. "It's safer this way. Trust me. Much easier this way."

The after-scent of his breath was sweet, almost smelling of fermented cherries. Melanie's nerves sparked with the realization that, if she wanted to get away, she'd not know where to go. Were they going in a circle? Or had they taken a direct route?

She tugged at his hand, stopping her forward momentum.

"I want some answers. I'm not comfortable, Naveen. This isn't what I signed up for."

She shivered. The damp darkness and smoky blackness covered her in fear. She already regretted taking the trip, and perhaps regretted trusting him in the first place.

"Ah, Melanie," he said as he attempted to wrap his arm around her shoulders.

She rebuffed him stiffening her spine and stepping away.

"The way out will be much more to your liking. Not at all like this. I'm here to ensure your safety. Not everyone knows how to do this."

He tried to get her to move forward again, but she resisted. Another attempt to wrap his arm around her failed.

"You are cold. The longer we stay here, the colder it will get. You are perfectly safe. But ask yourself this, Melanie. From what you know of Joshua, does it really surprise you that he would inhabit such a place? And wouldn't it also make sense he'd be very careful who was allowed into his inner sanctum? If you search your thoughts and perhaps your heart, my dear, I'm sure you'll see that is the case. It all fits perfectly. Don't you agree?"

"I want to go back."

"But we are nearly there."

"Where exactly? Now I want to know where before I take another step."

He did not release her hand but tucked it underneath his arm in an effort to warm her fingers. "I have arranged a private audience, in very safe quarters, where you can speak your peace and have closure, as you wanted. You'll be able to converse with him just as I'm talking to you now, Melanie."

"Even Josh wouldn't bring me to such a place. This is awful. It smells of—of—I don't know what. Dirt? Dust? Smoke. And cherries."

Naveen lamented her comment with a mournful moan, almost sounding like an animal in pain. "We've come this far, so allow me to take you just another ten steps. We'll count them, okay? And then we'll be there." He took a big step and began his sequence, pulling her along. "One—"

But she pulled back. "I asked you once. Where?"

"Do you always know where you're going, Melanie? You've come so far, and we're so close. But I'll humor you. I have found Joshua's castle, his secret chambers. This place you never saw, because it is his refuge from all the cares of the human world, and it's also protected from the minions of the Underworld. It is here he goes when he needs privacy, time to think. When he's troubled. But I must warn you, sweetheart. He *is* troubled. And you may not recognize him when you see him."

"So, you've spoken to him, then?"

"Not exactly. I've been told this."

"Is this because he is in danger?"

"Not at all. I don't believe he is."

"Does he know I'm coming?"

Naveen hesitated just long enough for Melanie to fully comprehend he wasn't really as in the know as he'd portrayed himself to be. "I'm afraid not. He will be surprised. I hope that, for your sake, it will be a pleasant surprise. But no matter, if you wish to leave, I'll be right at your side, and I will be able to take you home without any interference. From anyone."

Melanie knew she'd made a grave mistake.

"You are only steps away. Let's continue, One—Two—Three—"

She followed but hung back behind Naveen, suddenly fearful of what hid beyond the darkness. But her fingers had been thawed, tucked into his velvet coat. She felt the air begin to warm up. She attempted to sense Josh's presence but came up blank.

"Four—Five—Six—"

And then she could see a bright light coming from a sliver beneath a huge metal door. The light cast shadows on the building she'd entered. Stacks of wooden shipping boxes lay strewn, their contents busted out all over the concrete floor. There were articles of clothing, shoes, bottles of wine, candles, and a broken lampshade. Beyond the piles of open crates were a set of tracks.

"What train goes here?"

"*Used* to. These things, everything in here has been abandoned. You see? If you look you will find that the tracks lead to a stone wall. There is nowhere they go to any longer."

Before she could turn around, he completed the count. They stood in front of an old iron door covered in cobwebs. It looked like no one had been through this door in centuries. Naveen turned the oversized knob, a head of a lion or something wild, with a loop through its mouth. The sound of metal squealing hurt her ears as the large ring turned in Naveen's bony hand.

She heard a loud metal click, which echoed through the building. She heard flapping behind her as if a large bird had been startled. Naveen yanked on the handle, opening the door to a room filled with light from a fireplace taller than she was. A golden patina overlay everything in the room. Ornate, brocade tapestries covered a four-poster bed, matching curtains in deep crimson swaged with golden braided ropes pulling back, revealing a windowless blank space of wall.

It was a gentleman's bedroom. It smelled of rich earthy sweat laced with fine wines and musky cologne. No mistaking it. Josh's scent lingered in the air and made her spine tingle.

Melanie recognized several animal heads mounted on the wall she'd seen in his large home in Sonoma County years ago.

She'd forgotten about Joshua's taste for the finer things in life, his insistence on opulent displays of wealth and comfort. Although the room was now empty, there was no question in her mind that it did indeed belong to Joshua Brandon. Although she couldn't feel his presence, she believed he would come.

She'd found him at last!

Directly in front of her an ornately carved wooden door began to open, creaking on its old metal hinges. Melanie held her breath.

Chapter 3

JOSHUA DIDN'T HAVE much time to organize a spotter for the other side, someone to be there when his transport to the Underworld was complete. He'd purposely distanced himself from his dark angel crowd while he waited for the miracle of being human to really kick in.

Sadly, it never had.

He headed to former dark angel Jonas Starling's home to ask advice from his most trusted Lieutenant from the glory days. Josh had heard that Jonas was still in touch with some of his old crew. Perhaps he'd even have a recommendation.

It was important to make sure he was placed with a good entry team, people who didn't mess up the paperwork, so he'd have to wait a week or more in limbo, unable to leave the entry room. That could delay his reunion with Melanie, which he knew could be very dangerous for her. The Underworld was a maze of paperwork snafus with files and permissions for everything—rules no one followed but everyone required. That part of his former community he didn't look forward to, even though it allowed him to skirt around the edges and down shortcut tunnels to avoid being controlled.

He'd always told his "customers" to give him reading material he'd bring to them later, so they weren't bored, just in case. That also might take their minds off some of the sounds they might hear that could scare them, especially with newly acquired senses, including hearing. From experience, he knew this process sometimes ended poorly. He didn't want her to be afraid.

He mused on what he should choose for himself. Some magazines? A lusty novel or two? A book of love poems to brush up on before he met Melanie? Perhaps a couple movies on his laptop? He'd heard they'd created their own internet and social media now that dark angels had become tech savvy; those who had fingers and not claws, that is. He'd have to get a crash course from someone he could trust until the last vestiges of his feeble human cells were cast off like snakeskin. He couldn't wait to indulge in the firm, marbled flesh of his dark angel past, especially as he took his pleasure whenever he wanted.

Until he found Melanie, of course.

His mind was racing with all the plans he had. Where to go first. There was Helena's, the Blue Raven Bar and the Pink Pineapple with rows of nipple tasting every night. Nothing ever stayed exactly the same, so he was sure there were new places to be secretly frolicking, exploring, indulging and glamouring.

It would be a shame if the turning were difficult, long, or drawn out. God forbid the readers in the center would get too curious about him. He was probably still legendary in the Underworld culture. He'd heard the stories how some of them tormented and played games with the unsuspecting new recruits as they were regaining consciousness in their new dark angel form, much like morgue employees were rumored to do in the human world up top.

The euphoric transformation to dark angel left some extremely horny, ready to slut themselves or ram themselves into the first orifice, male or female, they could find. He didn't want to be forced to be someone's trophy fuck just so his entry didn't get delayed. The stakes were high, after all. If someone knew this, they might take advantage of either of them.

All this was a matter of logistics. He didn't fear the turning or his survival. It was how it happened that mattered most to Joshua.

Jonas' black Harley was parked on the front porch,

so Josh knew he was in residence. Before he could make it halfway to the front door, Jonas had bolted outside and ran right into him.

"Damn it, Josh. Where the hell you been?" Jonas barked in his deep monotone voice as he picked him up and held him over his head like a barbell.

"Whoa! Careful with the merchandise, Jonas. I'm starting to think you haven't been getting enough lately."

"Fuck that. Audray's naked and waiting for me inside. She'd like to see you too." Jonas blushed. "Not in that way, of course."

"Of course."

Joshua would have felt more comfortable tussling with Jonas if he'd already turned, but in his present frail form, he curbed everything and managed to slip out of Jonas' grip. He pretended he didn't hear the invitation to gaze on Jonas' lovely lady, which was the only smart way to handle it.

The guy still looked like a world-class wrestler. He had even more tats than before. He had more lines and less hair. He still wore it in a short snow-white ponytail. His beard was trimmed and was still as bright red as Josh had remembered.

Jonas grabbed him again by the nape of the neck as if he were a teen, unlike their days together where they ruled the Underworld and conquered everything they could. In those days, Josh had the gift of vaporizing, something he was hoping he could reclaim.

The front door was opened with one kick from Jonas' boot as he threw Joshua onto the rug in the middle of the living room floor.

Three young children sat, reading books by the fireplace. One was slightly taller than the other two and Joshua deduced he was the baby conceived in the Underworld before his parents were granted the same life sentence by Father. Humans forever.

But in Jonas' case, he'd prospered and obviously multiplied.

Josh scrambled to his feet, having entertained the youngsters who watched him right his clothes, giggling at their daddy.

"Look at you," purred Audray into Josh's right ear. She wouldn't let him turn around as she'd spooned behind him, rubbing her assets against his back, which was the safest move she could make. "I've often wondered what had happened to you, whether you shriveled up and wasted away," she cooed.

Josh felt her step back. When he turned, he could not believe how beautiful she had become in her human form. Older but somehow more alluring.

His eyes followed every fold in her red silk robe

cinched at the waist. "I always said there wasn't a being in the human world or Underworld sexier than a mortal woman with the memory of a powerful dark angel. You chose well, Jonas." He winked at Audray, who blew him a kiss.

"We're having another in May," Jonas proudly announced.

Josh felt a touch of melancholy and examined his boots, rocking back and forth.

He'd missed the company of those who understood the path they'd all been on and taken together. But one of them was missing.

Melanie.

As if he read Josh's mind, Jonas sat down and put one of the girls on his lap as she clutched her book. Wisps of her white-blonde hair glowed in the firelight.

"You're a lucky man, Jonas. I should follow your lead. As a matter of fact, that's why I'm here."

"You've found Melanie?" Audray asked, her eyes widened.

"I know where she is." Josh's long stare at Jonas made his friend erupt.

"Ah, fuck!"

His daughter giggled. Audray shouted at him. "Not in front of the children, Jonas. You get control of your mouth." She stood in front of him with her hands on her hips. It only elicited a wide grin on Jonas' face.

"Yes, ma'am. I will gladly accept any punishment you deem necessary, sweetheart. Just so I get the message loud and clear."

Audray tried to hold a stern expression as she gathered the three children together. "This is a friend of your dad's from his old job. Before your dad became a nice man and a decent father. Kids, say hello to Joshua Brandon."

Each of them did so. That's when Josh realized the two girls appeared the same age. "Twins?"

"Yes, this is Abbie, and this is Kate."

"Nice to meet you, girls."

"And I'm Adam," the older child said.

Joshua shook his hand.

"Now you three run along and finish your reading in the playroom while your father and I speak with our guest, okay?"

Audray was lovely, shuttling her little brood through the double glass doors and closing them behind her. Pulling her long blonde hair up, she tied it in a knot on top of her head, pointed to a chair across from Jonas, and then took her daughter's place on Jonas' lap. Her long legs crossed delicately, swinging, like the pendulum of an ornate grandfather clock, as if she was keeping her own time in another world.

She took his breath away.

The nice thing about her was that Audray had always been his secret weapon and was the best strategist he'd ever encountered. What Jonas had in brawn, Audray had in smarts. Street smarts. She'd grown up hard and mistreated as a young girl but never forgot her manners, waiting for her time to get even.

And she always did.

"I have to say that the sight of the two of you takes my breath away," Josh began.

"Bull shit. So what did you come for?" Jonas was urgent to get to the point.

"I need your help—well, advice really."

"You're gonna need my help sneaking back into the Underworld? Are you positive that's where she is?" he asked.

"Impeccable authority."

"So why did Father tell you this?" Audray questioned, her keen intellect figuring out his ruse.

"He wants that favor he asked of me the day I was made human."

"The guardians. He wants you to get his guardians back. Is that it?" Jonas squinted as if it was a huge stretch of a request.

"Yes."

"And to do that, you gotta go down under. Back

there. And while you're at it, bring Melanie back."

"Or return the guardians and stay down there with her if I cannot rescue her. I don't know what state of mind she'll be in. I haven't seen her in years. Occasionally, when I travel, I get glimpses of her in some nearby place. But since she was so angry with me when we parted, I never attempted to find her. I figured her life would be much better without me. But I wanted to."

Jonas and Audray nodded in unison, deep in thought.

"But now Father said she went there to find me, so I have some degree of hope, at least, that she wants a reunion."

"I don't see the problem." Jonas adjusted Audray so he could cross his legs.

"I don't know anything about the process in the Underworld anymore. How it works. I need a guide, a sponsor. Are you still in touch with anyone dark?"

"Um hum. I got a couple guys who could fix you up. When are you going?"

"As soon as you can arrange an introduction. They have to be solid, Jonas. No fuckups."

"Josh, you're like a brother to me. I wish I could do it myself, but there's no way now I would risk that. I've helped them, so they owe me a little. I keep on their good side, and they watch over the kids and my lady when I have to travel sometimes. They're pure, loyal dark angels. The best they come. They have no intention of leaving the Underworld, so you can trust them."

"They know the readers?"

"Yes, they'd know when to come through. I'm sure they could arrange for your passage when there are readers they can bribe." He delicately slid Audray aside and stood. Taking his cell out of his pocket, he made a call and walked outside on the porch.

"It is wonderful to see you again, Josh. I always thought it wasn't right that you and Melanie didn't stay together." Audray's smooth voice was soothing and professional. "You know we even sent Doris on a mission to find her for you after we found out she took off."

"Doris? The guardian cabbie?"

Audray nodded. "It was Claire's idea."

"I thought she was busy transporting guardians up and down to Heaven. Didn't think Father would let her go rogue, on a mission, for mortals?"

Audray giggled. "You know Claire has a special place in his heart. I think when Doris told him, he approved the mission. But, she couldn't find her. We looked everywhere for a solid month."

"We? You went with her?"

"Nope. She would check in with us. She had some

stories, I'll tell you that."

"Bet she was tempted to stay down her," said Josh, imagining the little red-haired crusty cabbie in the dented yellow cab. He remembered how she'd dropped off countless guardians in those days before Melanie. She was hard to miss, and Josh targeted her cab whenever he had time, following the new recruits on their first mission to save their human charges.

"Not Doris, Josh. She told me herself the human world was too complicated. That's why she carries that flamethrower in the back of her cab."

"I thought Father was going to make her give that up."

"Not on your life, Josh."

They both shared a laugh.

Josh's bright spirit was shattered with the remembrance of Melanie leaving him. "Someone told her a bunch of lies."

"Who? Doris?"

"No, Melanie. If I find out who and catch them down there, I'll take care of those little spiteful dark angels too. They messed with the wrong angel. Melanie isn't safe without me."

"I'm glad." She walked to within inches of Josh. Of all the women he'd wished he could have slept with, Audray had always been on the top of his list. But he enjoyed her friendship even more than he would have valued her as a paramour. Her delicate scent was unique. Slightly smoky still, laced with jasmine. Her eyes smiled back at him in recognition.

"You see Claire and Daniel very often?"

"All the time. The kids play together. Daniel also has done a good job of keeping her pregnant."

That sent a smile to Joshua's lips. He was genuinely happy for the former guardian he'd tried desperately to turn. His only failure. He put his palm on her shoulder. "Thank you for your help."

"I wouldn't be able to stop him. After me and the kids, he'd probably die defending you still. You know that, don't you? You were the brother he had missed for all those years."

Jonas barreled through the doorway. "They're on their way now. You got your shit together? 'Cause they'll take you down there tonight. Are you ready?"

"I've got nothing to carry except my phone and my laptop."

"Shit, Joshua. You can't use those there. But you can buy one. Go see the clockmaker. You know where he is, don't you?"

"The funny little mouse with all the bots?"

"Yup. He deals in all the parts down there. He has a corner on the wireless stuff and has his minions put phones and tablets together. They even have their own frequency sort of thing. Way beyond me. If he likes you or can use you, you're in."

"Sweet deal. Thank you."

Later, they heard the sounds of motorcycles approaching the house. Jonas headed for the bedroom. "Just a sec. I got something for you," he called out.

Josh heard him fumbling around, opening up drawers until Jonas returned just as the sounds of the engines cut out. He handed Josh a blue box.

"I kept a dose just in case. You take this, and you'll wake up in the reading room with no side effects, except one. You'll be right as rain. No sickness or headaches."

Audray giggled, burying her head in Jonas' chest.

"And what's that side effect?"

"You'll have the stubbornest boner you're gonna love. It'll drive you crazy, but it will last for about a week. Be very careful, though. Your whole focus is going to go south, and if you're intending to carry out a plan, write it down or you'll forget all about it. This stuff will make you forget your name for a while until it gets satisfied. But man, it works and you're gonna love every minute of it."

"Thank you, Jonas."

"Don't thank me. Bring me back another one to replace it."

Chapter 4

MELANIE WAS DISAPPOINTED to discover the person at the other side of the doorway wasn't Joshua, but an attendant who brought a tray with fruits and cheeses, and some bottled waters. She wore a white high-waisted smock like Melanie had seen Claire wear at one time.

After the young girl left, she asked Naveen, "Guardians, here?".

"No, former guardian. Sort of a welcoming committee. Have some food, if you like."

"So where am I, exactly?" She was confused that this place would have turned guardians and humans, if Naveen was indeed human, side by side.

"You're not exactly in the Underworld here, Melanie." Naveen's syrupy smile had faded. Melanie noticed how preoccupied he'd been with the doorway opposite the door they entered from, as if watching for it to open again.

"So, what is this place? I thought you said Joshua

lived here." She took a deep breath, hoping it would calm her nerves zipping around her insides like eels. Joshua's faint scent made her eyes water, and her breath hitched. Melanie wondered if the trace of him came from something in the room that had once been Joshua's, but she began to doubt that he actually lived here. The bust of a reddish-brown water buffalo she'd recognized stared down on her ominously, ready to pounce.

That can't be it. Melanie continued to scan the room, walking toward what she guessed was a double closet door. "Is this room part of a house or merely an apartment?" she asked.

Naveen was quick to notice. His body adeptly blocked her from opening the doors and no-doubt seeing an empty space, or see some other woman's clothes hanging there.

I'm not going to give you the pleasure of feeling my fear. In the year she lived with her former dark angel lover, she'd learned when to mask and when not to mask her feelings. There were times it was necessary to hide her thoughts and others when their non-verbal communication, even after his human conversion, enhanced all sorts of things, including sex.

But she commanded her insides to cool like snow.

And that made her shiver.

Naveen was dancing back and forth in front of the closet doors, trying to distract her, maybe even trying to read her thoughts.

"I asked you a question, Naveen. Does Joshua Brandon live here?"

The slithery beanpole looked like the cartoon character of a greedy banker who had taken the beautiful heroine hostage on the railroad tracks. He rubbed his knobby hands together and refused to make eye contact.

She whirled around and wasn't surprised when her path to the doorway from which they'd entered was blocked by the swift movements of her guide.

"I'm sorry. You can't do that," he quipped, folding his arms.

"Explain. I'm here of my own free will," she answered him.

"Indeed. Before you walked into this room, yes. But now, everything's changed. I haven't lied to you, Melanie. Josh will be back here, but I'm not sure exactly when he arrives. This is a place where he stays. But he has other places as well. You've seen at least one of them."

"So why the ruse about the permission forms then? Why even bother with all that?"

She remained careful not to show any flash of anger, but the need to scratch his eyes out grew stronger by the minute. Though Naveen was taller by half a foot, Melanie was certain she could wrestle him to the ground and get away if she had to save herself.

"Do you remember what you did to spare the life of your lover, Melanie? Do you remember what Peter gave you?"

She'd seen herself take the purplish-black pill in her dreams for years. She'd been willing to take the death dose to save Joshua's life. This time, she hoped she had completely bypassed this process by entering through the back door. Melanie thought she had found a way to cheat death and enter as a visitor, not a permanent resident.

"You assured me you had made arrangements to avoid what you called unnecessary complications, Naveen. I'm not ready to take a poison pill for Joshua, or any man. I've not agreed to this. And, unless my memory fails me, I have to willingly agree to abandon my human life to enter the Underworld. I've done no such thing. I came here to meet Joshua. I didn't agree to throw my life away."

"But what if it's required to see him?"

She stepped back, giving more distance between them. "One more time. I'm going to explain it to you one more time. This—this place—a place where he sometimes stays, is not in the Underworld, right? Yet you said you had permission to enter me as a visitor. So, if this is not true, then I'll either wait here for my meeting, or I'll leave."

Naveen didn't appear to take her seriously.

"You either have Joshua come here or you escort me back to the station and the tracks we passed on the way in. Is there some reason he's barred from coming here? Or being prevented? Is he ill or being detained?"

Her guide was fumbling, searching for words.

"Then I have my answer. I'm leaving." She started for the large iron door to the tracks.

He grabbed for her arm, but being more determined, she pushed him aside then kicked him in the groin. As he stumbled forward, he nearly grabbed her again before he collapsed onto himself moaning.

Melanie examined everything in the room, looking for something she could use as a weapon and discovered the fireplace tool with the sharp pointed edge leaning against the heavy stones of the hearth. She leapt forward, took the metal poker in her right hand and held it over her head like a bat.

"You get something to light the way and head through that door. I'll be right behind to make sure you get me back safely. If you dillydally, I'll make sure you get to feel the pointy end of this little device."

Naveen scrunched up his face, making him age nearly twenty years. "Ouch!"

Melanie was still frustrated at his lack of motivation.

From behind, another door opened.

"Melanie Worthington."

It was a woman's voice. The young, sexy and slightly Southern voice did not belong to someone she knew. She carefully turned around, keeping an eye on Naveen at the same time. The woman was dressed in red, the color of her lipstick. Her long black hair was severely cut in front into straight bangs. Her curvaceous form was poured into the form-fitting long satin dress. She wore large diamond-studded hoops that sparkled when catching the light of the fire.

She was just Josh's type.

Here comes the bad news.

The woman came forward, ignoring Naveen, who still was folded over on himself groveling. Melanie lowered the fireplace poker and decided she'd listen. Gulping in a deep breath, she addressed the woman.

"You have about thirty seconds to make some sense, or I'm outta here. I don't need a welcoming committee. I only came here to talk to Joshua Brandon. If he's not here, then I'll come back another time."

Melanie was proud her voice was firm and didn't rattle like her insides did.

"And you shall, very soon, Melanie. I can call you that, right?"

Melanie shrugged. She was getting heated by the blast of the fireplace, and her armpits were steaming.

"He's been delayed. I'm Cassandra. People around here call me Cass. I've been sent to make you comfortable and await Josh's return."

"When?"

"Pardon?" Her perfectly formed dark eyebrows rose as if it would help her hear.

"When will he be here?"

"Can I confide in you, sweetheart?"

"I want to know how long I have to wait here for him. Perhaps I should come back at another time?"

"Honey, I'm going to level with you. I'm an old friend of Josh's. If you know him as well as I do, well, you know he does pretty much whatever he chooses most of the time. So I'd get comfortable—take a little nap. The time will go by quickly, and you two can be reunited to your little heart's desire." She clasped her hands together like she was the soloist in a church choir.

Melanie searched between the disheveled form of Naveen on the floor, trying to right himself, and the woman who was probably one of Josh's converts and sexual partners. Her need to see him had suddenly diminished.

"You tell him thanks but no thanks. I'll come back when it's more convenient. And you have a nice day."

She turned, reaching the iron door, but the handle didn't turn. She tried it again and then yanked on it, pulling it as hard as she could. But the door felt as though it had been soldered shut. Unlike before they'd opened it, there wasn't a squeak or creak to indicate it had even let her in.

"I'm afraid it's too late for that, sweetheart. You best get ready to be here a little while. I'll bring you some more refreshments, if you like. Perhaps some spirits? We have wonderful blends here, and there is also our specialty drink, RedX. You just make yourself at home. Take your shoes off. Have some fruit and a little water and I'll bring you something stronger. Enjoy a bath or a shower if you want. I can get you anything you want. Some comfy clothes, a nightie, clean underwear. Anything you want. Just speak up. You can go anywhere you see here, just not outside this room."

"Excuse me?" Her anger kept her fear at bay. "I'm being held here against my will? On whose authority?"

"Well, that's just the way it's done. Those are our

rules, sugar. You're going to be wined and dined, entertained like you've never been entertained before. And you'll enjoy every minute of it. I promise."

Melanie couldn't believe what she was hearing.

"And who made up these rules? Is this a company building or something? A secret resort?"

"Oh, that's funny. I can tell I'm gonna like you." Cass winked as she pointed to her. "I'm sure Josh will be able to explain everything to you. He wants you to be comfortable and safe."

"And I'm not taking any black pill. I didn't agree to become a captive, either. Those are my wishes."

Cassandra threw her head back but didn't muss a single hair on her head. "You're just a little comedian, aren't you? I'll bet you're the life of the party. We love that. We really do."

"You're not addressing my demands."

"Oh, that's fine. I'll take it up with the Director when I see him. But you'll get the chance to see Josh first. Now, why don't you sit down, and lose those uncomfortable shoes? I'll get us some drinks for our parched throats. Fair enough?"

"Do I have a choice?"

Melanie's blood ran cold when she heard the lady in red's answer.

"No, sugar, you really don't."

Chapter 5

JOSHUA BRANDON RODE behind one of Jonas Starling's former team members on the man's shiny black customized Harley. It was a thrilling ride, made even more dangerous by the fact that the driver liked to max out the bike and thought nothing of swerving in and around traffic, even pedestrians when he chose to travel on sidewalks and across parking lots. Joshua was well aware of the fact that this dark angel was immortal. Unfortunately, if they had a crash, it could be fatal to his now human form.

"Can you drop the speed a little, sport?" he attempted to scream above the sounds of the howling wind and the specialized muffler attached to the bike.

The dark angel paid no attention to him, gunning the motor and nearly raising the front tire off the pavement.

Josh tried to settle his nerves, leaning forward, tighter against the angel's back. He hoped the man wasn't one of the modern creations who sported large black wings that seemed to sprout from above the shoulder blades. Such an action would surely dislodge Joshua from the bike and would certainly prove fatal.

During Joshua's three hundred years, wings were never the thing. However, the last ten years have brought interesting new scientific experiments. There had been sightings of constructs genetically reconstituted and patterned from old bodies dug up—creatures that had lived centuries ago. It was the stuff of legends, like some of the horror stories his father used to tell him when he was a child to make sure he stayed close to home, especially at night.

From his previous experience as a dark angel, he knew it was unnecessary that they ride their customized Harleys because most dark angels had the ability to fly, wings or no. But Joshua understood most of his former brethren had egos that defied logic. They thrived on danger since there wasn't much that could end their existence.

The biker slowed to avoid slamming into a recreational vehicle winding up the hillside from the valley floor below. By the time they reached the summit, a string of nearly twenty vehicles had collected behind. But the lack of speed gave Josh the silence he needed.

"Hey!" he shouted. He heard a growl registering he'd been heard. So he continued. "I'd like to get there in one piece, if you don't mind."

Again, there was no reaction from the angel.

"Did you hear me?" he asked. "My mortal heart is about to rip out of my chest. Take it easy. A few more minutes longer won't cause any problems."

That's when the biker decided to respond. "Jonas said you were in a hurry. Not so?" he asked.

"I don't like to go this fast. Please slow down."

Joshua couldn't hear it, but he could feel from the vibration coming from the angel's back that he had sighed. Gradually, the bike slowed to a more reasonable speed.

"Thank you. I'm grateful." Josh wondered if he'd soiled himself because his crotch felt wet. And if he had, that would be one more thing the angel wouldn't like.

He hadn't seen this part of the county before. There were portals leading to the Underworld all over Northern California that most humans knew nothing about. The land was often described as "Swiss cheese" due to so many tunnels and underground pathways leading straight there. He was amazed not many humans were aware of them. There had been legends of early German settlers to the valley who dug wine caves and ran into some of these tunnels, causing severe loss of life for the humans. But that had been over a hundred years ago.

Every entrance was protected by a building so that whoever was admitted could do so with anonymity.

Josh's re-entry was the most common. He'd take Jonas' big pill and then fall asleep once he was assured the two angels had everything arranged. The worst thing in the world was to be stuck in the theater, the readers passing judgement on his true death or arguing about the degree of coercion used and not allowing admittance. That could mean that he would still be dead, but not allowed to be revived as a dark angel.

Being stranded in the limbo land between both worlds was something he'd seen many times over the years. There were so many rules it was ridiculous. But no one enforced much of anything, but it could delay an entry. No one could remember who made the rules, either. The whole process was a mystery to everyone.

Joshua hoped for a few minutes to speak with the two bikers to make sure, now that they were close, all the necessary precautions were taken. He needed to hear that a reader was being paid to pass him through quickly. That he'd allow these two angels to carry Josh over the threshold into the Underworld and make sure his awakening was uneventful. If it wasn't handled correctly this could become what he used to call a *"true death without a future"* scenario.

He eyed several large buildings that suddenly appeared in front of them. One structure looked like a massive hospital, protected by guards that didn't look human.

"Is this it?"

The biker nodded and then began to slow down. The angel behind caught up and shouted, "We need to go over some of the rules, Mr. Brandon, so this can remain a seamless operation. Can we buy you a drink? An early supper?"

His stomach had been churning from all the coffee he'd had after he and Father had their talk. Except for Jonas and Audray, no one he'd had contact with today required food to sustain them. Josh was starved.

"How about a hamburger?" he ventured, his voice feeling the raw raspiness that came from shouting longer than he'd intended.

The second angel nodded his agreement. So they pulled into a diner that was just down the street from the large office building.

Inside, the space was decorated to resemble the style of an authentic 1950's burger joint. Pictures of muscle cars adorned the walls. Vinyl seats were meticulously wiped down. The host behind the cash register wore a white suit outlined in red. Josh held up three fingers, and they were shown to an oversized booth upholstered in a sparkly deep red vinyl. Menus were placed in front of each of the three.

Josh leaned forward and began the first of his many questions. "You've arranged that I'll come through one particular reader's portal, correct?

"No worries. We got it covered," said his chauffeur.

"Not sure if Jonas told you, but I was once very close to the Director." Josh thought about how to ask the next part he needed to know. He carefully dove into a huge plate of French fries that had been present-ed in front of them. They were delicious.

"I'm Noel, and your driver here is Spencer. We have a relative we're helping, a reader, and he knows what to do to get paid his regular fee, which is non-negotiable."

"Sure. How much?" Josh said, getting out his wallet and peeling off a thick wad of hundred-dollar bills.

"You better give him all of it," said Spencer.

"No fuckin' way. Besides, what the heck can he spend the money on down here?"

"Not here. It's when he stays in the human world, Joshua," said Noel. "He has some vices and entertain-ment needs that don't come cheap. But you didn't hear that from either one of us, okay?"

"Fair enough." Joshua held back some of his bills but gave the lion's share to Noel. He tore into his burger, orgasmically dripping in juices and melted cheese. "Hmmm." he mumbled. "These are great. You want a bite?" He offered the charbroiled perfection across the table but neither of the dark angels was interested.

"Inside, we have a gurney for you. We'll keep you comfortable until—you *did* bring the dose, right?" asked Noel.

Joshua patted his jacket pocket. "Right here."

Spencer inserted himself. "We're going to leave you alone for a couple of minutes while we go check to make sure everyone is where they should be. We'll be right back, and then we can go over the rules."

Josh stopped chewing and said with his mouth full, "Rules? What rules?"

"Jonas told us you needed to find someone right away." Spencer whispered, watching a stranger enter the diner and sit up to the counter within earshot of their table. If he was a dark angel, he'd be able to hear just as if he sat right next to Joshua.

"Yes, I was told she'd arrived or was arriving to-day."

"We'll try to get you sprung, but it could take two, maybe three hours. If she's new to the Underworld—"

Josh interrupted Spencer again. "She is."

"Do you know what gate she's coming through?"

49

asked Noel.

"No clue. I wish I'd been provided that information."

"Where do you think they'd take her?"

"Well, it sort of depends who brought her, doesn't it? But you have a communication system. You can call them."

"Josh, there are over a hundred portals within a fifty-mile radius of here. Half those guards are overworked and don't answer the phones. It will mean checking every single one. But I'll mention it to our cuz inside, and we'll see if he can put some feelers out."

He began to trust these two. The fact that Jonas had known them and worked with them for the past few years made them trustworthy as well. "What else do I need to know?"

Spencer chuckled. "You're gonna have one helluva boner, Josh. You'll be trying to suck your own dick. Jonas said to recommend a surrogate to get it polished off."

"No. I'll deal with it."

"Sure you will," mused Noel. "So that's why we're gonna follow along with you a bit. Just until you begin to get your bearings."

"Perfect." He quizzed them about some of his favorite haunts from his past life.

"Helena's still there. The Pink Pineapple is still there—"

"With the titty bar?"

"Oh yes. And the cages, the dancing—" Spencer turned to Noel and frowned. "What the hell are they called?"

"Well, they're bots. He made those sex dolls that dance, and, well, you know. Now, one of those wouldn't count. I mean your lady wouldn't mind because they're not human. Not even living. But man, they sure can perform."

"Practically suck the dick right off of you," added Spencer.

Both the angels giggled with glee until the gentleman at the counter turned around and sneered at them. After noticing Josh, he rose and came over to their table.

"Are you sponsored, son?"

Josh knew right away something wasn't quite right about him. He had a red ring around his lips from sucking on too much RedX—*The Elixir of Life*, as Josh had called it back in the day. His black jacket was soiled, and his hair was uncombed. He knew the man had a serious addiction, which was common. The first telltale sign was that the host stopped caring about his physical appearance until the red syrup corrupted the insides of a creature, eventually reducing them to a painful slab of meat and bones. Josh had always thought it a terrible waste of time, to be made immortal only to do oneself in with this drink. But he knew it had been created to control the population, since not much else was a danger to the angels below.

The strange man kept leaning closer until Josh could smell his body odor-drenched clothes and oily hair.

"Friend, this isn't my first rodeo. You're wasting your time."

With that, the stranger retreated, shuffling his feet in mismatched slippers.

After the gentleman sat down, Spencer leaned forward and motioned for Josh to do the same. "I'm not going to leave you alone with that dude. I think you'll have to just come with us and wait in the lobby, if you don't mind."

"Good idea," Josh said as he finished off his burger. He wiped his fingers on a wad of napkins and declared himself ready for his adventure.

He paid for the burger and drinks and headed toward the large square building in the middle of a plaza. This building hadn't been constructed when Josh was last in this part of California. He wondered who was organizing things these days.

"Do you happen to know of any guardians down here?" Josh asked as they walked.

"Helena has a couple. There's a bunch of them that stay in a big house together. They don't get out much," said Spencer. "They even wear uniforms, if you can believe it. Like a bunch of penguins."

"Say what?" Josh asked.

"Nuns. Like they're cloistered."

"It kind of makes sense, gentlemen, don't you think? I'm guessing something happened to their sponsors. Otherwise, how would they work their quotas?"

"We don't have quotas. We got so much business we're not in danger of shutting down. People are flocking to the Underworld right and left. The human world is getting to be a strange place. I think they do it to feel safe. Wouldn't you say that, Spencer?"

"Yup. Plus, I think most of those angels who know how to come back and stay living in the human world. But in their advanced state, well, they're more protected. And they can protect their families, some of them. Everything's getting mixed up, Josh. You'll see."

The glass doors to the lobby area opened on their own as the three approached. Josh took a seat next to a large picture window overlooking a grassy field. Someone had planned the building and grounds beautifully. Unlike how Josh remembered various buildings in the Underworld, this place was very masterfully created. It had a very calming effect on him. He'd been used to chaos and streets of quickly thrown-together housing and business structures. Someone had vision, it was obvious.

Spencer and Noel checked in with a receptionist professionally dressed in a navy blue business suit and white blouse. She pointed to a doorway, and the two disappeared into a theater-like auditorium. Josh could hear the tapes playing, the stories of their last final days and hours before they'd sought solace. That part had remained the same. The death had to be ruled a true death by suicide, not a murder. The readers were there to witness and pass judgment on them. And then to welcome them to their new home.

He fingered the blue box in his pocket. He'd wondered for most of the past ten years if he'd ever have the courage to return, even though he could feel himself attracted back to the dark side with every passing day. The news of Melanie just put him over the edge. It was like riding a bike to Joshua, a skill once learned he would never forget.

A set of double doors opened, and Josh watched as Spencer and Noel wheeled a hospital gurney out between them, heading in his direction. A white satin pillow was at one end, and a folded white fuzzy blanket was at the other, secured by straps attached to the underside of the gurney. The thin mattress was covered in a crisp white sheet, which had been pressed folded and laid out neatly to display its folded squares.

His blood pressure spiked a bit as he climbed up onto the gurney and allowed his head to fall into the pillow like sleeping on a cloud.

Well, I am assuming my more angelic form, even if it will be a dark one.

But it was the orderliness of it all that bothered him. His upcoming death was the admission ticket to the Underworld and the start of his true mission, as well as the place he would be reunited with Melanie. As Spencer pulled the blanket up to his chin, he removed the pill from the blue box and stared at it for a second. The chalky surface had tiny flecks of something that sparkled as he held the round dose between his thumb and middle finger.

"Would you like water, Joshua?" Spencer asked.

"Yes, please." He was surprised how compliant he sounded. Maybe this whole event wasn't going to be as big a deal as he'd built it up to be over the years in his own mind. Maybe this really was his predestined path and that's why he had very little resistance.

He placed the pill on his tongue and felt the object

melt onto the surface. Spencer handed him a crystal glass filled halfway with mineral water, just as he liked it, with a slice of lime wedged onto the side. The delicious water was refreshing. He thought he heard water lapping, and the sounds of ducks socializing.

He imagined he heard Father's voice saying farewell. "Bring them home, Josh."

He closed his eyes and began to feel sleepy.

There was music playing somewhere. Disgusting little birds chirped with other sounds of a normal day in his earthly form. Except today was no ordinary day.

He allowed himself to follow the suggestion he heard. "Relax. You'll wake up a dark angel. And you'll live forever," Spencer said.

"Yes," Josh whispered, falling into the mattress farther, his toes and fingers beginning to tingle.

Just before the blackness came, he felt someone cross the straps from under the gurney over his thighs, and then cinched them tight.

God, I hope these meds don't make me flop around like a fish.

He inhaled deeply, and in seconds he didn't care. He saw Melanie's face in his dream. "I'm coming for you, coming to the Underworld to join you," he told her telepathically just like he'd used to when they lived together.

He saw her open her eyes. Then her face became distorted, morphing into panic. Her mouth opened wide in a scream he could not hear.

Chapter 6

THE SHOCK OF knowing Joshua was not yet in the Underworld but was getting ready to give up his human life destroyed Melanie's whole plan. She'd totally miscalculated. Her meeting with Joshua Brandon could have taken place in the human world. She'd been tricked, and now the very person that she cared the most for—probably still loved, if she was being totally honest—was about to pay the price for her mistake.

Cass had talked her into slipping into some comfortable stretchy clothes after she took a long, luxurious shower to get rid of the filthy grime of the warehouse approach. Then she lay down for a nap, reveling in Josh's scent permeating both pillows. She still clung to her precious human life, but now she was faced with a dilemma.

Joshua is coming for me! Was seeing him worth giving up her mortal soul? Couldn't she see him in the human world? They'd co-existed as dark angels and human lovers for several months before she was forced to submit to the powerful director of the Underworld to save Joshua's life. Why couldn't they try that again now that they'd found each other?

Yet he was willing to sacrifice the miracle of his human life given to him by Father himself just to see her. He was risking much to contact her. Would he feel it was all in vain if she left, returning to the safety of her human life? And then what if she couldn't leave this place? What would that mean?

Please don't. Stop. You don't need to do this, Joshua, she tried to say to him telepathically. She listened for an answer, holding her breath and wishing on everything she could that he'd hear her. But nothing came back. Again, she sent out the warning.

Joshua, please let me know that you are all right. Don't do this for me.

But the longer Melanie waited for an answer, the more her chest filled with sorrow. With her hands covering her face and her knees pulled to her chest, she wept, mourning the happy reunion that now might not occur and hadn't needed to occur under such dangerous circumstances.

For although she was happy to see him again, she knew he would realize in time that he had sacrificed something that he didn't need to. She had damaged him and, in doing so, mortally damaged their relationship.

She became suddenly sleepy and wondered if Cass put something in the cold drinks she delivered just before her shower. Melanie wondered why. If true, who was the catch and who was the bait? They'd each traveled to the Underworld with the intention of finding the other. But she felt the presence of some dark hand also controlling the outcome.

Am I the target or is Joshua?

Her eyelids felt so heavy. Edges around her field of vision began to turn dark, the picture inside growing smaller and smaller. Was this some sleeping medication or had she been slipped a lethal dose of some kind? She didn't have the energy to be angry. Soon, she couldn't move her legs then her arms. Her breathing slowed. She fell into unconsciousness.

Joshua!

Melanie woke up on a gurney and for the first several minutes, she was grateful that someone had come to her aid and taken her to an Emergency Room or hospital. She heard voices whispering all about her. The air was chilly, and lights surrounding her gurney were too bright, making it so she had to cover them with her palms. Someone took notice of her movements and was at her side.

"Melanie, how do you feel?"

"I am—I'm not sure. I'm cold. Where am I? Did someone take me to a hospital?" She kept her palms over her eyes to shield herself from the light. "Please turn them off. They're too bright."

"Oh, yes, that is a side effect of the medication I gave you."

Melanie felt the lights dim. She rolled on her side and tried to look in the direction of the voice. Instantly, she recognized Cass, dressed in a white lab coat.

"Are you a doctor?" Melanie knew it was a ridiculous question, but her ability to think logically was greatly diminished. She felt like she's been sleeping for a hundred years. "What medication did you give me?"

Cass gave a gentle laugh, brushing the hair off Melanie's forehead. Although she normally would've thought it to be an act of kindness, she knew something terrible had happened.

"A cocktail. A very special cocktail. I know, it's a lot to get adjusted to. But trust me, you will."

"Get used to?"

"Feel your body Melanie. Don't you feel more energetic, younger? Aren't you a little bit more excited this very moment to see Joshua after all these years?"

The shock of what she had just gone through

dampened her desire. But there was no question every cell in her body was firing on all cylinders, like she'd been connected to a low-level electric current or energy field. She was humming, buzzing to a cadence completely familiar, yet exciting and brand new. It wasn't an unpleasant experience at all.

"Where is he?" Melanie asked. She longed to show her new body machine to Joshua, and to feel him through her new eyes.

"I believe you'll be reunited shortly." Cass picked up a clipboard and began perusing several sheets of paper. "Now I need you to sign a couple statements. Then you'll have to be photographed, and you'll soon be attending some orientation. I am your sponsor, Melanie, which means I am responsible for your transition, that is until Joshua can take over." She smiled, internally musing. "I have no doubt he'll get right on that, too."

Melanie tensed, scrambling to attempt to sit up and then stand, but Cass firmly held her shoulders and kept her in seated position on the gurney. That's when she saw the others. There were several occupied gurneys each with an attendant, covered in white sheets the same as her own. Only one other individual was stirring awake. His attendant was speaking to him in hushed tones, but Melanie caught the full drift of his message.

Welcome to your new life.

"What is this place?"

Fear had taken some of her voice away. Her pitch had risen, constricted by the tension she held at the back of her throat. Her heart began to race and instead of her usual response to fear, which would be an upset stomach, she began to hear a high-pitched buzz as her ears suddenly became super sensitive to every little sound around her. Her cheeks were flushed, her nipples had hardened, and she felt moistness in her panties. All of this embarrassed her.

Cass' eyes registered recognition as the seconds ticked by. That's when she knew that she had crossed the line.

"I'm in the Underworld!"

"That you are, my dear."

"But I never agreed to this. You *took* my life. I never gave permission."

"Well, you passed the readers. And you were informed, I believe, that it was impossible for you to leave. I understand you intended to visit Josh, and you knew that the Underworld was where he was headed. So, it's really a technicality. I mean if I were to walk out in front of a truck, I didn't ask the driver to hit me but I placed myself in the path of the truck. What do you suppose is going to happen?"

"But that's not how it's supposed to work," Melanie insisted. Joshua told me—"

"Oh yes, there's the rub, isn't it? You see, Melanie, Joshua was a legendary storyteller. He bent the truth every chance he could, and that's why he was so successful as a dark angel. But you don't honestly believe that all the lovely things he told you—all those beautiful things he might've said during your pillow time—were one hundred percent true, do you?"

"I absolutely do. He's not the only one who has told me about some of your rules. And you've just broken a big one."

Cass sighed and sat on a metal chair that was standing near the head of the gurney. "I'm sorry to have to tell you, but we don't really have an appeal process here, Melanie. I mean, we don't have a court system or someplace where you can apply for redress."

"But you have rules. I've been told about all your rules, and how things are done."

Cass smiled sweetly. "Well, I think it's best if you just accept a few things. And then we can see what we need to do to keep you comfortable. Our goal is to make it so you have a certain quality of life here. And you will have Joshua to consult with, of course."

"But I've told you. I didn't agree to this."

Melanie held up the clipboard. "We're about to fix that my dear. I'm going to have you look over the agreement and then we'll see about getting something a little more stylish for you to wear. These are more like relaxed fit pajamas. Not designed to make a stunning first impression. I'll make sure you also find some makeup."

"I'm not signing anything." Melanie crossed her arms and surveyed the large room. It was designed in a very minimalist fashion with tall ceilings, light grey wall, and polished granite floors. But the room was a box with no windows and felt more like a large gym. There appeared to be only one way in or out, and that was through a large set of glass doors leading to a darkened hallway. Above the door was the electric sign:

Theater is in operation.

The letters were spelled in bright orange neon tubing, almost as if it led to some kind of a television or radio station on the other side.

"Your viewing has already been completed. That's what generated the paperwork." She held up the clipboard again. "I need to go over several things first before we introduce you to the viewers and get you photographed."

"Viewers?"

"You see, that's why they always assign a sponsor.

Well, think of me as a friend. And if you're successful reuniting with Josh, perhaps I won't be needed at all. It happens both ways, Melanie."

"Yeah, a friend who murdered me." Melanie's voice echoed throughout the room and she noted Cass' uneasiness with her outburst.

"I hope we aren't going to have any problem with you Melanie. It goes much better if you just accept what is. You're going to have all eternity to get yourself settled into a routine that in time, you will learn to enjoy. And you're getting to do it with someone you love. Not everyone here has that option."

"I didn't even get a chance to say goodbye to my parents. My friends. This is so unfair."

"Some people feel this way for a little while. However, after a few days it's very rare that a new recruit is displeased with the outcome. I think it goes back to the fact that there really is no appealing this decision. So, people do learn to live with it. And as for your parents, they will be able to see you again, but you'll be in your immortal form. They'll just think you've suddenly become more beautiful. You'll be able to hear them on the other side of their bedroom door. If they whisper to each other, you're going to hear it. You might find you'll be able to protect them better with your heightened senses. But all that will happen in time. First, we need to get you processed."

"When will I see Josh?" She was still insisting on terms on her behalf, even though she knew the battle had already been lost.

"Soon, I believe."

"He's recently arrived too. Isn't that right?" Melanie queried.

Cass frowned with a very slight nod and a wrinkled brow. "I'm afraid dealing with Joshua is above my pay grade. I don't know everything about his entry, but I am aware of the fact that he would like to see you very much. Surely that must mean something to you?"

It meant the world to Melanie. She was going to need his help. She had so many questions, and everything about what had just occurred was so entirely bizarre. Now she understood why he was so secretive of his life here. He hadn't really told her a bunch of lies. He just had been very good at avoiding an answer.

As she leaned forward, Melanie felt a sharp pain at the back of her neck just at the top of her spine. She fingered a lump with a small ridgeline the width of her forefinger. It felt like someone had applied several stitches.

"What happened? Did I fall or get injured?"

"I was just getting to that. That's a microchip. It's just in case you get lost."

"What do you mean, get lost? I thought you were going to be here to guide me?"

"That's true, Melanie. But for your own good, your actions will be monitored. We only do this for a short period of time in the beginning. Again, all of this is being done for your protection. We want this to be as seamless as possible. Besides, your body will help absorb the chip in about a month, give or take."

"Who has access to the information in the micro-chip?"

"Well the Director for one, and he has a small staff. After a while you'll forget it's there. It's standard procedure now."

She spent the next several minutes going over dis-closure statements which Melanie had been very familiar with in the human world. As the former owner of a boutique flower shop and gift store, she was well-versed in leases, agreements and building code viola-tions. She remembered Cass' admonition on rules and regulations. But she also understood that there was no way she was going to be released from this room without signing the paperwork. So she glanced over the material and affixed her name to all five pages.

"I have the chip number noted here on your copy of the contract, for your information."

"That's fine. Now I feel like a papered dog. Honestly, isn't this a little over the top?"

"It's standard here, like I said." Cass checked the pages to make sure the documents were valid.

"You know, Cass, I admit it's painful to lose a favorite pet. I think the analogy is perfect. Only question for me is, who's pet am I? Do you know the answer to this?"

Melanie watched Cass' reactions carefully. The dark angel was adept at covering up all the gory details and only highlighting the good. In her normal state, Melanie would have been furious, stubborn and miserable. But the fact was she felt fantastic in her new dark angel body, which added to her overall confusion. And that made it hard to be angry at the woman.

"You forget, Melanie, I've seen this before many, many times. You'll learn to trust me as we get acquainted. Now, let's move on."

Cass helped Melanie off the gurney, tucking the clipboard under her arm, and showed her to a large dressing room, one wall covered in floor to ceiling mirrors. On two other walls were hangers full of women's clothing labeled by size.

"You may choose whatever you like here. You can try it on or take it with you and return it later if it doesn't fit. I suggest you take several things. We also have a wonderful collection of lingerie which most people seem to enjoy very soon after their arrival."

In spite of herself, Melanie blushed.

"Once you've made all your selections, we'll greet your readers. Only very briefly, okay? And then would you like to return to Josh's room to await his arrival?"

"Was that really his bedroom?"

"Yes. Although he hasn' been with us for many years, his quarters remained intact, and available to him once he returned. We'll find you two a suitable place in time. But in the meantime, you won't be bothered there, since most people don't even realize it exists. It is like exiting through the back door. I think that was the appeal."

Melanie ignored that comment and turned to the clothes. She selected several silk pants, and colorful embroidered tops also made of silk. She found some satin pumps. Cass had been completely truthful about the quantity and variety of unusual and sexy lingerie. She selected everything in black. She'd never seen such high-quality hand-made items.

With her new clothes folded in front of her, she allowed Cass to direct her through the doors to a small theater seating. Plush burgundy rocking chairs were sparsely occupied by a variety of people, some sporting outrageous costumes. The garish bright colors made the room look like a sit-down Halloween party, even with the dimmed lighting. Most of the crowd stood and clapped for her debut. Scanning the audience, she saw no evidence of Joshua or any of the dark angels she'd met previously. The smiles were fake and wide. Several men and women blew her kisses, as if pretending it was a festive occasion, masking the fact that she had sacrificed her human life and probably her mortal soul.

A photographer motioned for her to stand beside Cass for a picture, and then he took one of Melanie by herself. All this was done at the rear of the theater under the watchful eyes of her audience.

It felt so wrong in so many ways that, when prompted, she quickly followed behind Cass and breathed a sigh of relief when they were outside, standing in an enormous covered courtyard that looked like a football dome. She'd made it through the gauntlet at last. Her libido began to remind her of her upcoming meeting. She loved the way she felt and her anxious expectations, unlike when she was human, only gave her strength and did not make her sick.

Cass motioned for her to continue through another wide corridor.

"So those were the people who approved of me, you said? Just what exactly did they have to approve?" Melanie asked.

"I'm surprised you don't know the answer to that. They are witness to your ascension, your desire to join us."

"Wouldn't it technically be called a descension?"

"It's not how we think of it, Melanie. If you ever doubt this, just see what it feels like to exist inside your new body. You'll be smiling before too long, trust me."

They walked slowly through a maze of tunnels, all clean and very brightly lit. At last she recognized the outside of Josh's distinctive bedroom door. Cass placed Melanie's hand on a small keypad the size of her palm, and the doors opened automatically.

"I took the liberty to make it available to you. I'm assuming Josh would approve."

"So you have access to this room, then?" she asked.

"Well, I'm your sponsor," she said as she held up a key card.

When they stepped inside, Melanie understood about the extra sensory powers she now had. Before, the scent of her former lover had been very faint.

Now it completely overwhelmed her.

Cass showed her the counter-sized built-in refrigerator she had thought was cabinetry. Opening it, she demonstrated its contents. "You have waters, wine, several bottles of our specialty liquor made right here, some fruit, and some cheeses. You won't be hungry, but some still have that need to fill up, so this will take the edge off."

Melanie was speechless.

"I will ask about getting you a phone, so we can communicate, just in case you'll be alone here for any length of time. Before I take off, would you like me to bring you anything else at all?" The sound of the refrigerator door closing with a sucking sound made Melanie jump.

"You're sure he will come?" she asked. The delicious feeling of being a virgin, ready to have her first encounter was a fantasy she allowed to play in her head. Her senses were becoming more heightened with every passing minute.

"Melanie, I don't think there's a chance anything could keep him away. The two of you will not be disturbed here. Joshua knows his way around enough to find you whatever else you need. And I think he has friends here too. No doubt he's going to be contacting them first. It's good to have allies here. Very smart too."

Cass' words fell like an ominous warning. Melanie shivered.

After the angel left, Melody sat on the bed and wondered about all she'd been told. This upcoming meeting wasn't at all what she'd expected. A tiny sliver of fear coursed down her spine as she waited. Her new clothes called to her. She removed her casual clothes and carefully put on the gorgeous black lace set that was a perfect fit. Selecting a black pair of silk pants and one of the embroidered tops, she slipped them on carefully. Then she stepped into her black velvet pumps and sat on the edge of the bed to wait. She felt like she was six, waiting to perform at her piano recital.

She didn't have to wait long. The door opened, and Joshua stood before her, leaning against the frame. Suddenly, she found it hard to breathe. The sight of his black curly hair tied back into a short ponytail, his knee-high, highly polished black boots, and that casual way he looked at her, sporting just the hint of a smile, made her heart race. Her flesh immediately desired his touch. It was a hunger she'd not felt so intensely before. She was melting under the anticipation of his fingers exploring her body in that ritualistic way he did things, and he seemed to know what she was thinking. She wanted to hear what was going on inside his head.

She used their familiar and long-practiced line. *Penny for your thoughts, Joshua?* she sent out telepathically.

He slowly closed the door. Pictures of their beautiful lovemaking filled her head, images from his memories.

I have thought of nothing else all these years, he sent back to her.

Her body warmed as he slowly traversed the Oriental rug, making his way over to her. His eyes noted everything, drinking in her essence like a starved traveler. As he got closer, she noticed he wasn't wearing the light-weight black raincoat she'd always seen him in before. He'd selected a jet-black velvet waistcoat over a bright white shirt.

"Oh, sweet Melanie. My thoughts are worth so much more," he whispered.

As his dark eyes studied her, his forefinger lazily traveled across her lower lip. Suddenly he was leaning into her, his fingers cradling her head gently at the sides. He pulled her to him, inhaled, and pressed his lips against hers as she felt the heat radiating from him ignite every dormant flame in her body. Every worry and snippet of fear suddenly disappeared as their tongues mated. What replaced her fears was the heavy jolt of erotic pleasure that set up an even bigger craving. She recognized it as that part of her life she'd been missing for years.

She was desperate for him as their lips slowly parted. The desire reflected in his eyes proved he was feeling the very same way, and it left her tingling all over.

"I have dreamt of this meeting just about every night since you left. There has never been a day when I did not think about you. Think about trying to find you. I didn't want to stay away, Melanie. I wanted you to come to me."

"And so I have," she whispered, closing the gap between them again, stealing another long kiss.

Joshua closed his eyes and took in a deep breath. When he opened them again, she saw his tears. "It was not this way. I didn't expect this," he continued as his voice broke.

She touched his tears with her fingertips, brushing them away. "Oh Joshua, I am so sorry. We could've done this another way. But I didn't know. They lied to me."

"I know. I completely understand, sweetheart. You probably feel responsible for this."

She was puzzled with this statement.

"The truth is, I was sent here by Father. This was to be my destiny anyway." He placed his palm against her cheek as she gently laid her head into him. "But I didn't want this for you."

"Yet here we are. And I'm never going to leave your side again. I am where I belong. Forever."

Chapter 7

TWO THINGS HAD come back into Josh's life. Although he was hesitant to return to the Underworld to do Father's bidding, a part of him understood that this was probably where he belonged. As his body awoke from the slumber and death of his mortal soul, he reveled in the transformation of his new form. He watched as the muscle mass in his arms grew. His thighs pulsed with extra energy. He had a keen sense of taste and smell. He was powerful, even more than he remembered being before.

Melanie trembled under his touch. He found himself being careful, moving slow, listening to her breathing and noticing how the fine hairs on her neck stood out as his lips approached to taste her sweet pheromones. Though he was careful, every place he kissed her blushed an erotic shade of pink. He nuzzled her breasts, unable to get enough of their opulence, while examining the texture of her nipples. His tongue rubbed back and forth while he watched her face, even turning her head gently, begging her lovely dark eyes to open for him, as her legs spread and her knees hugged his hips. He wanted her to see in his face the pleasure he felt inside her thoughts.

It's never been sweeter, my love, he told her just before he pushed her chin up and claimed the underside of her neck with his kisses.

He felt her question, and his erection grew even harder.

"Your body is so familiar to me, Melanie, and yet it still feels brand new and exciting like the first time." He whispered against her lips and open mouth. He held his arms around her upper body, pressing her breasts into him as she arched, moaned, and wrapped her left leg around his right hip. He pressed his thigh tight against the lips of her sex and gently rubbed her mound while she rode him.

The scent of her sweet juices began to drive him wild. He quickly broke away and plunged his tongue deep into her channel, taking her lovely elixir as his bounty. With her knee up over his shoulder, she was fully accessible to him, and he took advantage, first inserting one finger then two, then his thumb. Adding his tongue, he bit her little nub with his teeth until she flinched and giggled with pleasure, hiding behind her hand.

Melanie always had that innocent aspect to her. She was an experienced lover, especially after her years with Joshua, but she could be alluringly shy and virginal too. The combination made him want to be strong but careful. He loved watching her awaken to his touch.

Her fingers laced behind the top of his head, squeezing his ears and then following his jawline with her probing fingers. His hand guided hers to touch herself, helping her squeeze her clit, and then he inserted her fingers inside her as she began to pant. He withdrew her hand, lapping and sucking everything he could get.

She rose up, reaching for his cock, and he pulled back to let her take him. A groan escaped as he watched her touch, fondle, and then bury him deep inside her mouth. She delicately worked her magic until he felt like he could levitate. He was spellbound, enjoying the persistent way she'd do anything to make him happy as she took the lead and took full control over his body. He read her thoughts as she pulled him deep down her throat all the way to his stem, powerless but to give her everything she demanded.

With her tongue curled around him she sucked, moving up and down on him. Exploring his tip with her playful tongue, her lips turned up in a quirky smile as she teased him. He covered her hand with his own, bringing his body up to balance over her. Together, their hands placed his rod at her quivering opening and gently moved his head inside the warm, moist lips of her womanhood. He didn't force himself on her, but he watched her as she pushed him across the threshold, her innocent eyes and lines at the top of her nose showing her desire for him. She pushed him farther, moving aside her nether lips, and then squeezed his balls.

He nearly filled her on the spot.

Quickly, he grabbed her hand, pressed her arm above her head on the pillow, and laced his fingers through hers. Adjusted his shoulder to take the weight of her bent knee, he slowly plunged inside her, angling up, nearly lifting her off the bed with his hardness.

Her expression of rapture forced him fiercely deep, desperate to claim her, to wipe out the lonely years between them forever.

Her head thrashed from side to side as he moved against her warm channel, pressing as far inside as he could go and then slowly withdrawing. Back and forth their bodies mated, as she melted, resisted and then softened with the strength of his command.

Everything in the room disappeared as his passion demanded she give him every single cell of her body, claiming every moan coming from those luscious red lips. He took her hard, furiously increasing the pace, and then gently let her down just before she could reach climax. Then he began it all over again until finally she fell over the edge of control and shattered beneath him. Her nails dug into his buttocks, demanding he go deeper. Her channel clamped down with selfish demands on him, begging him to spill and milking his member. He held her hips tight against him as they locked against in a long, groaning release, sharing the pleasure, joy and intensity of their joining as strong as any earthquake.

He whispered an apology, sorry that he couldn't help himself. Yet he was still pulsing, unable to finish and sad it had been so short. Her message back to him was not anything he could remotely understand.

Jonas had been right. He felt like he could fuck day and night for a week and then do it all over again the next week. His fingers caressed her as she cooled down, tweaking her nipples, rubbing her hips, buttocks and thighs while coaxing her libido back into action. He wasn't nearly done.

When at last she began to realize there was more, her eye widened. He loved seeing it written on her face, her willingness to open up to him all over again as he played her body's sweet tune.

He swiftly came to a sitting position, bringing her up and over his thighs. Positioning them both while still seated deep, he then gently released her to balance on his lap. She braced herself on his shoulders and moved her pelvis against him, giving just enough pressure to allow resistance to enhance the movement of flesh on flesh. He guided her body up and down on him until he felt her begin to tense again. He slowed way down, holding her firmly when reaching his full seating. Angling his hips up, he rose to meet her halfway, even lifting her on his member where she balanced. And then he bounced her, picking up the pace while she first began to giggle and then lose control.

Just before she started her spiral to orgasm, he leaned forward, pulling her legs up over his shoulders, and pressed her back into the bed. Coming hard and deep, his knees lifted her buttocks so that her channel remained wide open, defenseless against his still widening member seeking plunder. Her full surrender was a thing of beauty as she told him hundreds of times how much she loved him.

It was a tantric trance, the power of all of him—his hands, his fingers, his tongue, the muscles of his lower belly and his thighs. Every part of him lived to bring her to the peak of arousal. He was able to curl up and sit inside her mind, pleasuring her flesh on the outside but still experiencing it as she felt it on her insides. The double pleasure of giving and receiving, being the deliverer as well as the object of desire, engorged him, filled his heart with pure joy.

At last, he whispered, "Melanie, only this will heal my flawed body, the demons in my soul. You bring me courage."

Her beautiful eyes filled with tears, blending with those he shed upon her flushed face. Her lips were sweet. Her soft skin was smooth as glass. Her breath became his breath as he claimed all of her.

She whispered, "I was a fool. We wasted all those years when I left. It was totally my fault."

He stopped her with more kisses. "Shh. We don't talk about loneliness, because all that's over. We talk about what we've found again. I was the fool. Now this can last forever. I'm going to explore every possible way to keep you satisfied so you won't even think of running away from me."

He released her legs, positioning them to wrap around him again so he could stay inside, and rolled them to his left. He stroked the sides of her cheek with the backs of his fingers, watching her eyes sparkle, and then followed the descent of her body as it sunk into the bed. Her eyelids grew heavy, and then he watched her fall asleep.

Night night, he said to her telepathically.

But she was already out.

JOSHUA HAD SO much energy he found it difficult to doze off, so he spent the afternoon watching her, protecting her rest while enjoying the closeness and warmth of her body. He had that satisfying feeling he used to have in the old days when he was bedding mortal women, leaving them near total exhaustion and almost to the point of not being able to walk afterwards. Still, he had preferred guardian angels, those delicate creatures Father had spent so much time creating to perfection. He reveled in watching their faces bloom with the knowledge that they were in fact sexual beings and could feel the passion of sex, enjoying it even as their souls were lost in the forever of the Underworld.

But Melanie, was unlike any other. Even as a mortal woman there had never been a sexual partner who could come close to wearing him out, but if it were possible, Melanie would be the one. Now in her new dark form, she would spear his heart with a fatal needle, binding the two of them together with golden thread for all eternity.

He placed a kiss on her forehead and felt the crease

at the bridge of her nose deepen. But she remained asleep.

He loved everything about his new body. It was all he had hoped for and more. He'd wondered if he would be as powerful, if he would feel as good as he used to. He'd spent years pushing it out of his mind, the wonder of how his former self had never truly gone away as if that old body had been ripped out, leaving behind old roots that had taken sprout, and then perhaps withered on the vine. It was always an unexplained mystery during those lonely years after she left, the mortal years he spent searching for meaning in his life he could never find. Waiting for those roots to come back alive and take him over.

He now realized after only a few hours as a dark angel again that he'd been right, that this was probably the form he was intended to take and live his entire existence with. Up until today that had always caused a problem because the only woman in his life he'd fallen in love with was mortal and wouldn't be able to join him on that journey. It left him questioning, empty and very sad.

He wasn't sure Melanie would feel the same way in time. But he remembered his lessons from trying to keep her happy with his new mortal legs, his mortal needs and his lack of superhuman abilities as an ordinary man. It was more than his ego talking, a matter of genetics. He'd been created differently than most other people, and perhaps that was why Father hadn't hesitated to send him back. Maybe he was truly the force for good when he was manifest as a dark angel.

All the great thinkers and theologians will have a field day with that.

But that's what tickled him. He smiled up at the ceiling as he remembered everything about his first life here. In those days they had a quota, which gave him a mission and purpose, goals to set and records to shatter. He did it so he would never be subject to anyone who sought to control or use him. He had lived under countless directors, some of them very powerful and drunk with the need to dominate everyone in their wake. He wasn't a warrior. He wouldn't challenge them. He stayed clear out of their way and tried not to attract attention.

He stayed busy. He never failed. He used his passion for those young guardians as the fuel, his ticket to safety in a very chaotic world. And so he was granted more freedoms to leave for weeks and months at a time even. He explored the human world, looking for clues to unlock the secrets of Father's creations.

This time, there were many new things to discover.

It wasn't hard to notice the changes. He'd strolled past some of his favorite hangouts from before. Some had been updated. Many were torn down and replaced with huge, modern buildings made of steel and glass. Yet everything still appeared to have been patched together, just on a grander scale with bigger parts. Whoever was running things—and perhaps it was ruled by committee now—they'd been on a massive building program.

He'd never seen so many large and beautifully designed glass and steel structures, including skyscrapers and multi-story government offices that weren't even imagined in the centuries before, mostly because the need hadn't arisen. But now, murals with sayings extolling the virtues of the Underworld were painted on those complexes as well as on billboards. Banners were plastered all over, adorned with pictures of famous Underworld citizens he did not know or recognize. Their quotes praised the directorate for helping lift up its people, for protecting them from the evils of mortal men. With quotes such as, "I never had purpose before but now my life has taken on new meaning. I live to serve my brothers and sisters in the Underworld."

In short, there wasn't much he recognized of this brave new world.

Someone had figured out a secret they were still trying to get correct upstairs. They were trying to harness the power of the dark forces in the Underworld, not by limiting their movement and commanding them as a king, which was what used to happen, but by motivating the masses to do their bidding. And with the steady stream of new recruits—including men and women who had prospered in the human world, had made fortunes, and led movements and companies, only to fall—to *willingly* fall—there was plenty of talent to go around.

Joshua didn't understand this at all.

Temptations of the flesh still ranked high amongst the new recruits. That was the only thing anyone down here used to care about: The freedom to live in excess. Well that, and the possibility of living forever in a perfect body without illness or pain with freedom to do whatever the hell they wanted to do. Underworld society now conducted itself in a more organized and cooperative fashion, benefitting all, instead of every man or woman for themselves. Jonas' men explained some of this to Josh, but until he saw with his own eyes, he'd discounted it.

In short, the Underworld was getting its shit together.

There had always been a healthy collection of races

from all over the human world. Hundreds of languages, even obscure ones that had died out upstairs, flourished here. And that made sense, Joshua thought. They had centuries to teach each other and collectivize in a group. Since children below the age of consent didn't land here, a loose-knit family had developed over centuries. New recruits were taught and were added to the group. It gave them a place to belong.

A dark family of soulless sponsors and alliances.

He'd also seen a marked increase in the number of people wearing the color red. Red X had always been popular, but now he saw red paper lanterns floating everywhere. Some of the large banners posted from the buildings resembled those he'd seen on television when he lived in California. There was an abundance of statues of Jahn, Confucius, Ganesh, and many other gods and idols posted in windows randomly scattered throughout the seedy downtown, lit by red tea lights and often adorned with leis of flowers.

It appeared the whole place had gone through some cultural transformation, adopting some form of communal practices that incorporated elements of Egyptian, Indian, Oriental, and Polynesian cultures.

In fact, Western civilization was not represented at all. Perhaps someone had designs to change the history of not only the Underworld but the human world as well. He wondered whether or not there had been an actual purge.

Melanie began to stir. Soon, she'd want all the answers to questions he hadn't yet discovered for himself. He used to be able to maneuver around the distractions and bumps in the road for a smooth, luxurious life in the Underworld. Now, everything was out of his control.

And the person he loved the most, his very reason for existence, was counting on him to guide the way.

This is the definition of Hell.

Chapter 8

MELANIE FELT SO normal in her totally supernatural, immortal form, that she even found herself considering whether or not the Underworld would need a flower shop. She still missed those days, enhanced by the memory that that was when she met Josh.

He was still beside her in bed, his arms wrapped around her softly, just in case she had any thoughts of running again. It brought a smile to her face, being captured in this erotic way.

"What's got you all smiling and pink this morning, my love?" he whispered as he kissed her.

His hair had grown longer since their meeting years ago, several ringlets pulling across his forehead, intruding on those sexy dark eyes.

"You're going to think this is funny, Joshua."

"Try me."

She refocused on the ceiling again and began. "First of all, I feel wonderful. And I'm sure all of this has to do with it."

"Define *this*." He drew out his words, hissing like a snake.

She kissed him and then watched as her fingers stroked the softness of his lips. "I say that because there's a part of me that feels this is so normal. Like of course I would want to live this way. Whatever was I afraid of? I wonder why you never told me about it all."

"Because I wanted to preserve your humanity, Melanie. Above all else, that was the only way I could think of to protect you."

"I understand. And there's probably a lot I don't know that would have me concerned—"

"Yes, there is. And we'll have to have a talk about that very soon."

She was timid about asking him but overruled herself. "The thought just came to me, do they need a flower shop here?"

Josh rolled over on his back, his head touching hers, sharing the same pillow. She could hear as well as feel his heart beating.

"You know, I can't think anything like that has ever been done down here. It's just not what people do. Things don't *grow*, they get made or created. There's lots of things that are different. Since nobody ages, growth isn't anything this world focuses on. Growth is seen like a fungus, a flaw in the human world." He turned on his side to face her.

Melanie was surprised with his seriousness, waiting breathlessly for his answer.

"But there are stores here, things are bought and sold and made. Services are provided." He wiggled his eyebrows up and down at that comment.

She suddenly wanted to know what he was blocking her from seeing. "What was that about? Tell me, Joshua."

"Everyone's buying or selling at some point. At least that's the way it used to be. Everything is social, relationship oriented. Those who survive here have something they can sell and of course, that means—"

"Services for all kinds of pleasures," she continued for him.

He propped his head on his elbow, thoughtful. His right hand stroked her chest delicately, outlining each areola, pressing and pinching the rosy peaks of her engorged and throbbing nipples, lacing down the sides of the soft puffs of her tender flesh in a subtle suggestion that perhaps they weren't quite ready to get dressed. She was in need of a little distraction as well.

She matched his ministrations and teasings with bold touches of her own, her fingers wandering down to dark and dangerous territory. Her subtle response was noted, and fully acted upon.

EVEN THE SHOWERS were fun, she thought. He told her there was someone they needed to meet, an inventor who sold computers and cell phones that would operate in the Underworld jurisdiction. He refused to even attempt to describe his workshop. She would feel, he promised, that she was in the middle of a Disney movie.

The tiny inventor's shop, dimly lit from within, contained moving parts and faces of timepieces. Peeking inside was like watching fish in an aquarium. Small animals and carved figurines of clowns, kings, moons, and stars moved along little tracks, everything in motion, casting various shapes and shadows against the walls and the sidewalk in front of the shop. The painted, antique-looking letters in the window read *"Clockworks Unlimited."*

A second sign hanging from the shop door that read *Out of Time.*

Melanie pressed her face to the glass, examining the myriad of moving things, and spare parts tucked away on shelves and hanging on small chains from the ceiling. It looked like a combination toy store from a gothic novel where the villain liked to lure unsuspecting children inside, to the workshop making prosthetics, artificial legs, arms and apparently heads.

"He makes robots?"

"Yes, he does. I was introduced to him by my friend Gideon. People go here when they want to add something or remove something."

She watched as a flock of mechanical little blue birds flew in a cloud, whirling and turning just short of hitting the walls of the tiny place, occasionally knocking something off a shelf. They landed together, chirping and bobbing their heads and tails just as she'd seen real birds do.

"These are amazing."

Some annoying insects, gnats or something similarly sized, noisily flew over her head. Melanie attempted to swat them away with her hand.

"Oh dear. You didn't tell me they have bugs here. I suppose next you'll tell me they have snakes."

"Not that I've seen," he answered. "But don't hurt them. Look more carefully at how they fly."

She noticed that they were shiny, and minute particles of their bodies lit up when they came in contact with light, reflecting back on her. "Are those mechanical, like the birds?" She was astonished with her find.

"Bots. He makes all sorts of things like that. He sends them everywhere to listen, record, and bring back information he needs. He knows everything that goes on here. These little things can slip under or over doors, crawl through cracks in windows or walls. They're hardly noticed unless they get close enough for you to hear their high-frequency buzzing."

"So, I wonder if they've checked us out."

"Most definitely. See, here he comes." Joshua pointed to the glass door window at a little man coming toward them. "They've told him of our arrival."

The shopkeeper wore overalls and a white apron, stained with smudges of brown even something that looked like blood. He had rounded shoulders and wore huge dark-rimmed glasses which magnified the size of his eyes double. Even with that, he squinted and pressed his nose against the glass, looking at them both. He quickly opened to them. The bots followed, remaining in cloud formation over their heads. The blue birds alighted and then found other shelves to perch. The clockmaker still blocked the doorway.

"Joshua Brandon. I heard you got a special dispensation from Father and were now living up top. Was my intel incorrect?"

"I'm not proud of the fact that I seem to have preferred the lifestyle down here. And there were some aspects of the human world I screwed up big time."

The little man cackled, then placed his hands over his mouth as if he were a little boy about to say something naughty. Melanie liked him instantly.

"So this is your lady then, Joshua? And you have a name dear lady?"

"Yes. Melanie. And you are?"

The shopkeeper peered up at Joshua and grinned. "They call me all sorts of things, depending on what someone's position is. But I'm Manfred, and I don't shake hands anymore. Besides, no one likes to." He held up his right hand, which only had two fingers, and a thumb.

"I know just the man who can fix that," said Joshua.

"I don't trust anyone I've trained yet. Maybe someday I'll stir up the courage to attach them myself. But the thought completely disgusts me." He leaned forward toward Joshua. "You've set up home here, then?"

"We've only just arrived yesterday. We have a lot of sorting out to do."

Manfred seemed disinterested in his comment, stepping very close to Melanie and examining her, his glasses distorting the size and shape of his eyes, revealing every single vein and imperfection. He smelled horrible. Melanie worked to close out those thoughts just in case he had the telepathy.

She noted the bandage on the top right corner of his forehead, and his complete lack of hair. The rest of his forehead was sparsely populated with purple and brown warts that look like half-sized pomegranate seeds. Everything about him was distracting. But she allowed him the perusal.

"Joshua, I'm surprised. She is not a guardian." he said grimly.

"How can you tell?" she asked.

He shrugged, the clips at the top of his overalls dangling a bit as he laid his arms back down. "When you see as many angels down here as I have, you develop a sixth sense for them. He used to never hang around anybody but guardians or, I guess I should say, former guardians."

"I am considerably changed," Josh added.

"Well, come on in. She's harmless." He looked up at Joshua again and continued, "But I guess you already know that." He closed the door behind them. "So let's get to what brought you here. I can guess. Do you want me to?"

His eager face was filled with mirth, delighted at the prospect of some kind of game. "I'm going to say you are looking for a telephone, a little handheld model so the two of you can talk. Is that correct?"

S. HAMIL / SHARON HAMILTON

"You got it. And I was also told you sell the internet and might have an extra laptop I could purchase?"

"The service is free, but the laptop will cost you."

He turned, and the two of them watched him waddle down the aisle between several shelves holding boxes of parts, wires, springs, and dozens of clocks. In fact, it was almost hard to hear with so many ticking clocks around. Most of them had movement, either wagging tails or eyes sliding from side to side or speaking to the clock next to them. It was surreal seeing timepieces act like little pets, but that's exactly what Melanie thought they were. These were his little angels, his creations.

The shop held other moving parts as well. Pieces of metal from kitchen utensils, pots and pans, gardening tools, and even small motors were blended with clock faces. The hands, also made of various materials, inched up or down or around in circles, causing a chain reaction of other moving parts like an antique conveyor belt powered by some inscrutable source. She noticed the mechanical devices measured and told time in a variety of ways, but nothing appeared to be causing the movements except weights and momentum from other moving parts. There didn't appear to be any electricity or gas present. The only light appeared to be from flickering candles.

"Do you make all of this yourself?"

The clockmaker stepped up onto a wooden stool and began searching through a bin. He wasn't at all careful with the contents, finally coming up with a bright pink cell phone, holding it up to Josh's face.

"You like?"

"I'm not keen on it. Maybe for her. Do you have something less obvious, less girly?"

"Oh, Joshua, have you no sense of humor? Big, serious, masculine angel like yourself has to play games sometimes."

Melanie blushed, and the clockmaker's eyes widened in recognition. "I am not endowed with the gift of telepathy, but I just saw a very racy scene. I suspect you have a dirty mind, young lady," he said as he pointed to her. "I myself have been working on my own program, but it's been unsuccessful so far. Someday, though. You watch."

Melanie knew better than to bet against the little man.

Still gripping the pink cell phone, he stepped down off the ladder and handed it to Melanie. "Not for you Joshua. I presume you want something fairly double alpha male then?"

"Something plain. Something that will disappear"

The clockmaker perused him up and down, his

hands gripping his non-existent waistline. "Oh. I see. Well, I might have one or two things that you might like. Come this way please."

He waddled farther down between the rows of equipment, until he came to the end of the shelving. Then he turned left and stepped through a glass door that opened with a huge sucking sound. He stopped abruptly, and both she and Joshua nearly ran into him from behind. He closed the door again.

"I forgot. This is a sterile room. You have to wear facemasks." He pulled two disposable masks from a jar next to the doorway then slipped rubber gloves over his hands but didn't require Joshua and Melanie wear them. After all three of them were masked up, he opened the door again.

The brightly lit room did indeed look like a surgery center. Two gurneys, covered in white paper, stood side-by-side. Hanging from several chains draped from wall-to-wall were limbs, both arms and legs, and several pairs of angel wings, one white, and several black ones. He also had a pair of *shiny* black ones that appeared to be huge bat wings, not the size that Melanie had ever seen.

Josh made sure her curiosity didn't result in her touching them. "If you see any creature wearing a pair of these, you stay clear away. Understood?"

"Absolutely, Josh."

"So, I was playing around with some of my things here and one of my students kind of made me laugh. Let me see what you think of it."

Next to a clear plastic bin of what it appeared to be soft body parts, he slipped something quickly in his apron. Although Melanie couldn't really tell what was inside, she determined that it held creature parts in cellophane baggies, flesh colored for just about any skin tone in existence, from light brown to almost black, from very pinkish to nearly cloud-white color, and everything in between. Something even looked reptilian green. She stepped forward trying to see through the plastic and noticed one extremely large penis.

"Oh my God. Are these real?"

The clockmaker cackled again, wringing his hands together and shaking his head. "I have so much fun showing these to ladies, you know. I do specialize in that kind of elective surgery. It's quite popular. But no, these are prosthetic pieces. Although I have dabbled in sex organ transplants, but again, it's a brutal surgery with less than stellar results. Who wants to go through all that pain just to have something hanging down there that you can't use? Who cares if it's big if it doesn't work?" He shrugged.

Josh said absolutely nothing.

"My ordering department thought they were ordering doll parts. They forgot to ask what kinds of body parts they were. You can't trust anyone online anymore. Ridiculous how much extra stuff I have because it's just too damned difficult to return it." He sighed and shook his head again.

Melanie was surprised to even be having this conversation, but she noted Joshua's scowl.

Manfred pulled out that something he'd slipped into his apron and handed it to Joshua. It was an enormous black penis with a keypad installed in its shaft.

Josh wouldn't touch it. "Looks extremely painful," he muttered, watching Manfred turning it around in his hand. "That's a little too high profile for me. I'd even take pink over that one."

"Well, if you like pink I've got a lovely set of—"

"Excuse me, but I would just like a regular phone. I don't need anything that looks like a sex object. Like I said, I don't want to draw any attention."

"Oh geez, I thought you of all people would be a little adventurous with your choices." He exhaled, rounded his shoulders as if dejected, threw the cell phone prototype on the counter, where it bounced all too realistically. Then the little man continued, "So if it's vanilla you want, it's vanilla you get. I got an order of surplus military phones, and we re-designed them since all their circuitry was blown out in an EMP blast somewhere." His fingers flew through the air, demonstrating wherever it occurred, it had occurred in the human world. "They come in gray or Army green. Pick your poison, Joshua."

"I'll take the gray."

"Okay, so you want the no-flavor vanilla one then?" He opened a bin drawer stuffed to the top with gray phones, rummaging through all the devices until he picked one. "I think this one is perfect. And it will connect with your laptop, which I'm going to get for you as well."

Joshua accepted the nondescript phone. "This is perfect. Thank you."

They followed the little man into a warehouse through a doorway in the back of the surgery room. The warehouse was easily ten times the size of the shop, chock-full of parts in bins and hanging half-made robotic men and women that looked so lifelike, Melanie wasn't sure but some of them weren't sentient. They hung suspended from the ceiling, their eyes looking down as if watching the three of them pass by.

All of a sudden, movement to the right caught the corner of her eye. She grabbed Josh's arm. Several lifeless bodies swung from side to side, having been disrupted.

"Tabitha?" The clockmaker stooped, looking for something crawling on the floor.

"It's his cat," Josh whispered.

Surprised, Melanie had not seen a single dog or cat or other animal except birds since she arrived in the Underworld. She heard a rather timid meow as a large gray cat—well, at least she was shaped like a cat, but she had no fur—stepped blithely into their paths.

"She likes people," the clockmaker added. "When Melanie stooped to pet her, the clockmaker gently pushed her hand to the side. "She looks more gentle than she is. She actually enjoys biting people, has a taste for it, so don't give her the chance no matter how many times she rubs up against your leg, okay?"

"Got it." She watched the cat treat Joshua with great affection, almost teasing him to respond.

"No way, Tabby. I've seen what you can do and it's not pretty." The cat sat down and regarded Joshua, angling its head as if trying to understand his words. Then she got up and ran down the aisle, causing the little bell affixed to her collar, to ring wildly.

"You behave Tabby!" The little man confided, "She chases my birds, and when she catches one, she completely kills it. She leaves springs and screws and tiny electrical components strewn all over the floor, and it can be dangerous. Someone could trip and fall."

"Does she ever catch real birds?" Melanie asked.

"Oh, she's a house cat. She never goes outside. But with my little cloud strike group? You know, the gnats? Well she tries to go for them too, but that's because they tease her all the time. Like most real cats, I'm told the fun is in the hunt, the eviscerating parts, making a mess, just because she can."

Josh squeezed her hand. "I told you, Melanie. And we haven't even seen half of the stuff he's got here." He addressed the clockmaker again. "Where are all your staff?"

"Well, Joshua, you probably don't know about all the changes here. My people have to go to so many goddamn meetings, I think they're down at the government offices more than their hours working for me. We're terribly backed up. And I'm the only one who seems to care."

"So tell me more about that? Where is all this coming from? I mean, is it something a new director has imposed on everyone or what?"

"That son of a bitch Peter that you offed several years ago was really the last human director. Oh, he had his devices and his flaws, but once you steered clear of some of his pet projects, and pet people, it wasn't so bad." He winked at Melanie. "You remember him, don't you?"

She shuddered, "A horrible man."

"Well, he was predictable. I like predictable people. They can be evil as hell, but you can count on them for consistently doing the same thing every time. I like order. I know that sounds ridiculous considering nobody's really paid any attention to this place for the centuries I've been here, but now you have this new People Police. They require that people who work for entrepreneurs like myself need extra training in leadership. Why? I'll never know. It doesn't do a damn thing around here except make everybody argue. And I hate arguing. I'm the boss."

"Who are these People Police and how are they selected?" Joshua wanted to know.

"By election. Except everyone cheats. It's just like the way the director was chosen. Except in those days nobody really wanted to be the director. Everyone wanted to just go do their own thing. I don't see anything wrong with that."

"I always wondered what's the use of an election if everybody cheats? That was never anything I wanted to do."

"That's because you're smart, that's why. People who strive for power and then get it wind up spending all their time trying to defend their position. They are at war with everyone. It's not for me."

An hour later, Josh's new compact laptop was safely tucked into a new shoulder bag. They said their good-byes.

Manfred's parting comment was to Melanie. "If you need a little enhancement, you know, up here," he demonstrated holding his palms over his chest, "come on back and I'll fix you up with a really nice pair. You'll love them."

Chapter 9

J OSH HAD ARRANGED for a meeting with Spencer and Noel. The designated meeting place had been a large open air pavilion surrounded by rings of little hand carts selling everything from RedX cocktails to T-shirts and souvenirs. So many of the dark city alleyways had been torn down Joshua had to work on himself several times to remind his brain that he was still in the Underworld, not in an inner big city back alleyway in the human one.

He thought it was funny Melanie was so preoccupied with the clockmaker's last comments. He pretended not to notice as she checked herself out when they passed a window or something shiny, trying to slip in a glance to examine the reflection of her upper torso, checking out the size of her chest.

"Don't do that honey. You're perfect. I don't want you any other way."

"But why did he say that?"

Joshua cursed silently to himself and then realized

she could hear his thoughts.

"Sweetheart, it's because he's an asshole, because he just wanted to mess with you. He does it to everybody. Don't worry about it."

But he could see she wasn't going to give it up so easily. She kept peppering him with questions, asking if people did this sort of thing all the time, whether the breast enhancement would last if she went back home to visit her parents, if there were risks involved. Whether it would hurt her chances to nurse if she got pregnant.

"Pregnant? Who said anything about getting pregnant?" he asked, feeling his powerful blood coursing through his veins. The rocket in his pants, however, was interested. He resisted the urge to threaten castration to get his pecker to behave.

"Well, it happens. Two people who spend as much time as we do, fucking ourselves silly, why not?"

"Because, Melanie—" He looked into her eyes, which had started to tear up. He was so fucked. He'd not thought out everything that could happen. Just when everything was turning out so well, there was this. Something she couldn't have.

"I can't?" She moaned, dropping her hands and fussing with them in front of her, turning around to look at their environment and who could be watching.

"You've got to stop reading my mind, Melanie. We can't do this all the time. In bed, it's another thing. But out here, who knows who could pick something up?"

"It's an excuse. I said *pregnant,* as in having your babies, Joshua. It's not subversion or some political statement. It's about becoming a family."

"Except that doesn't happen down here. We don't grow things."

"I'm not talking about *things.* I'm talking about a child, Joshua. Don't you want that?" Her hands were solidly on her hips now, her scowl deepening.

His only saving grace was to livestream his swearing to himself at ten times speed and hope that she couldn't catch up.

"Why are you so against this? I think it would be incredible," she insisted.

"This is the fucking Underworld, that's why. Do you see children running around here, Melanie? Do you see babies in prams being pushed by nannies? No. No one has children here. We're all infertile, and that's the way it should be. It has nothing to do with what I want, it's the way it is."

Even her little act of defiance, the way she tipped her chin up as if accepting a blow she could withstand, was kind of sexy. He knew the conversation could be quashed in bed, and that's the only place it should be brought up.

"Don't do that to me, Josh. I won't be fucked silly."

That was funny. Really funny. She was so incredibly wrong, but he tried to mask it. Maybe she just ignored him and his lack of tone deafness to her needs. But she needed to know the realities of their lives now, and there wasn't any sugar-coating it, either.

He could tell she was trying to calculate whether all these things were something she should consider. It completely ruined his good mood.

"Melanie, you were given this perfect body. Don't screw it up. We have a very good thing going here. I might like to be three or four inches taller, but do you think I'm gonna let that little lizard stretch my bones? Do you think I'm nuts?"

"But Joshua, seriously, is it done here?"

She wasn't going to let it be. He finally had to tell her the truth. Exasperated and hoping it would quell her curiosity, he answered her truthfully. "Yes, honey. Breast enhancements are done. But I think people should only consider that sort of thing if something is really wrong, if they came here deformed, or had surgery as a human. He could help that person feel better by making them more beautiful in their eyes. But to the people who really love them, it doesn't matter. And there's nothing wrong with that. But you, you're absolutely perfect. I wouldn't change anything. And you know that no one gets pregnant here, but that doesn't mean I love you any less."

"Jonas and Audray did." She was softer, but she did raise a good point.

"And I honestly don't know how that happened. He was a royal stud. That was his job. Maybe it altered him, somehow. I dunno. But no more talk about this, okay? I'm open to researching this further, but not now. Now you have to get climatized to this place. We have to get our bearings, our focus. No more distractions, unless we're—" He delved into the images of them making love in the shower, in the bed, doing things she'd never done before, how they explored her boundaries, and how it thrilled him he'd found no barriers to anything he wanted to do with her. He could live this way forever. He really could. He felt her soften further.

The pink blush on her cheek told him he'd been right. It was just like in the old days up top, when he used to glamour the guardians and women he wanted to bed. But this was bending the love of his life so that her experience was enhanced, so she would feel free to fall in love with him more and more every day. It was for the good of both of them he did this.

He put his arms around her with a hug, then held

her face between his hands, and kissed her.

"Don't ever doubt me again, Melanie. You don't have to do anything to be more beautiful in my eyes. I'm telling you the truth. Honest."

But even in the Underworld, karma existed. As they strolled past several of the vendor stalls, a group of women from Helena's house approached them. He knew every single one of them. Two of them were former guardians but the rest were part of Helena's stable when he'd been a regular there. He had intended to explain some of these things in time, and soon, but it wasn't anything he had wanted to do today. In front of these women. Now it was being forced upon him.

The look on Melanie's face broke his heart. He knew if he tried to pull her away, they'd chase after them. He felt her inquiry, asking for an explanation. He sucked in air, and prepared himself for blood and guts.

"Ladies, this is Melanie, and we are very happily together." He saw the effect his abrupt conversation termination method was working as each of the women, formerly smiling, stepped back as their eyes widened.

Finally, "She's darling, Joshua," one of the ladies said.

"Very pretty," said one of the other girls, a redhead,

who walked around them both. Joshua felt like a piece of meat at an auction house.

Melanie was checking out their skimpy clothing, the bright colors in their hair and the heavy makeup. He knew there wasn't anything lost on her.

Their perfume was hitting Joshua squarely in his nostrils, inflaming his sinuses and it didn't take long before he started to sneeze. Annabel, one of the former guardians approached Melanie.

"So, this is your first visit here?" she asked. Somehow Annabel had managed to keep her angelic looks. Her turning had been an especially pleasureable one for Joshua, but he clamped down the images, covering them with photos he'd seen of dead decaying animals.

Everyone, including Melanie looked back at him with varying degrees of disgust.

He shrugged. "Come on, ladies. She's only been here a little longer than a day. This is all new. Leave her alone, please," Joshua pleaded.

"Annabelle, don't." one of the tall ones in the back came forward and yanked the young former guardian a good distance away from Melanie. Joshua couldn't remember her name, but he did remember her size. She was taller than he was, nearly larger than Spencer, and that was saying something. With her deep, husky voice, Joshua took her for a former opera singer. She was very statuesque, gorgeous, and been in high demand due to some of the things she could do with her vocal cords while pleasuring men with her mouth and tongue.

But Melanie wanted to speak up. "I'm not a child, Joshua. I'm not so naïve as to think you weren't different then. I've always been prepared for your past creeping up to greet me."

Several of the ladies let out titters, however subtle.

"I'd like to do this in private," he continued, "because I told you before, there's a lot I need to explain."

"She's smarter than you are, Joshua. She knows the score, don't you, sweetheart?" the big girl barked.

"Would you have some respect, please?" he pleaded.

The ladies began to laugh.

"Those are some pretty choice words coming from you, Josh," one of the ladies said.

For a very brief second, Joshua worried that this life with Melanie in the Underworld was never going to work. He abruptly shut down those thoughts, but it was too late. He felt the pain of her emotions and the worry in her chest. If he hadn't been so intent on enjoying their bedroom frolicking, he might have done a better job of orientating her so that something like this didn't blindside her so completely.

He'd been a fool again. The only thing he could do was apologize. *To everyone.*

He grabbed Melanie's hand and turned to face her. With the audience of his former playmates looking on, he humbled himself and meant every word.

"I am so sorry—"

"Stop," she said, placing her fingers over his mouth. "Like I said before, I knew who you were when I came here to be with you. This is what comes with all that." She removed her fingers and took his hand. "Now, introduce me."

He was shocked with her reaction. "Um, well, let's see, we have Annabel. She was a former guardian. Cloe, and, gosh, I can't remember all your names."

He put his hand to his forehead, uncomfortable, trying to bridge the gap between his past and the present he wanted so desperately to save. The women were cordial. He'd done nothing to incur their wrath. He needed all the allies he could get, so he was grateful for their civility. He was well aware this meeting could have had a different result. They each took a turn to introduce themselves and then gave a long stare Joshua's way, perusing him again. He wished he could read their evaluations, but he couldn't.

He waited until the group sauntered past them and continued on their way down the wide boulevard. He didn't look over his shoulder to watch them, but Melanie did. He was glad her focus had changed and thoughts of having surgery and raising an impossible family were now completely replaced by a whole new set of questions. He vowed to have a discussion this evening, making sure he covered all the bases he needed to, for her safety and for the preservation of his mission.

Melanie squeezed his hand. "I'm not giving up on those ideas yet, but yes, now I can't get out of my head that—" she stopped, and he paused right alongside her. "You *slept* with all of them? Every one? Don't lie to me. I'll know if you do."

"And do you also want to know how many times?" He continued walking, pulling her along behind him. He hid his smile from her but not what was in his heart.

Melanie wasn't lagging, but she turned around again, watching them, and then whispered into his ear, "Thank you for that thought."

He drew his arm around her shoulder. "It was during the time of my life when I didn't have someone like you in it. You know that."

"What did you mean about allies?"

He stopped again, the comment shaking him. "You have to stop doing that."

"I don't want to."

"But it's eavesdropping. Can we make some rules about it then? Otherwise, I don't feel you trust me."

She stared at her feet. "Fair enough. I shall try."

Josh breathed a sigh of relief. Then he added, "By allies, I meant down here it's very political. Always was, but everyone acted like it wasn't. Now, with all these shifts in policy, until I get my bearings and figure out who the power players are, we have to be very careful."

"Don't you think it's like that up in the human world, Josh?"

"You forget. These people are all flawed. They were flawed before they came here. Not many would ever want to be redeemed. Not like it is up top. People are striving, trying to give their lives meaning, trying to become better."

That's when he realized that perhaps he had misjudged his decision to do Father's bidding. He considered himself one of those striving to improve humanity, perhaps protect it.

"You wouldn't ever want to be a guardian, would you?"

"You have to stop that. I really mean it, Melanie."

"But you are a good person, Josh. I see that in you. If you're trying to hide it, you certainly don't bury it very deep. I think those ladies knew about that all along. It really doesn't surprise me."

He liked hearing that, even though he wasn't totally convinced.

NOEL AND SPENCER were sitting at an outdoor cafe, two glasses of RedX sitting half-empty in front of them. Josh pointed to his laptop case as soon as they spotted him. Noel drew another chair from a neighboring empty table and all four of them sat together.

"Good deal," said Spencer. "I'll bet he overcharged you."

"Like any good businessman would when there's no competition. Come on, Spencer. Get a life!"

Spencer wrapped his arms around himself, annoyed.

"He actually gave me credit. I'm to bring him the cash within a week. But no. I thought he was fair, especially considering giving me the terms and my lack of options."

Spencer returned a lopsided grin then downed the rest of his drink. The next grin he gave showed his teeth to be red. Josh knew it was for Melanie's benefit.

"Sorry, man. I couldn't help it. You bring a beautiful, innocent thing like her down here, Josh, and, well, it makes everyone crazy."

Noel frowned. "So how are you holding up,

ma'am?"

Josh thought his attempts to be charming were laughable.

"I'm—I'm fine. There's been a lot to see. Kind of mind blowing, really."

Spencer started to chuckle, his huge form making the chair groan beneath him. "You gotta be crazy bringing her down here. She doesn't belong. I'd get the hell out, if I were you."

Josh had to stop him. "You don't understand."

Spencer checked the surrounding area and then leaned onto the table. "She's not safe here. Neither one of you are safe. What, you thinking of playing house here or something? This is no place for you two."

"I have a job to do."

Noel added his thoughts. "You came here to save her. Now that you've found her, you should go."

Josh was concerned with their attitude. "Is there something you're not telling me?"

"The whole place knows about her and you. Did it ever cross your mind all this was not a coincidence?" Spencer said, drilling a look that told Josh he was serious.

"Who's been talking to you?" Josh asked.

Noel shrugged. "Word is, people want information about you, Josh. And her. Lots of interest in her. I was asked several times if you guys had connected yet, and what your plans were."

"Who, dammit? Who is it that is asking all these questions? I've been gone over five years. I didn't think I'd be forgotten completely, but why anyone should care what I do here?"

"They have these meetings, and they talk about how we're one fellowship. And," Spencer stopped himself, so Noel finished for him.

"We're encouraged to report people who are outliers." Noel studied Melanie. "They don't care for those who don't kneel to authority."

"But whose authority? That's what I'm trying to get out of you two?"

"We have a board of directors, made up of different trades and districts. Recruitment, commerce, quality of life—"

"Energy conservation," Spencer inserted.

"Fuck me, Spencer. Energy conservation? Here?"

Both dark angels nodded solemnly. Joshua couldn't believe his eyes. "So what does this have to do with me?"

"We have no idea." Then Spencer added, "Except I'm supposed to report to the chairman tomorrow morning for a session. I'm considering leaving tonight."

"It's that bad? Did you know this when you picked me up?" he asked the angel.

"There wasn't time. Except we told you things were changing."

With the crumbling walls of Josh's expectation happening all around him, he decided to get back to the point of this meeting.

"So where do I find this dorm you said the guardians are in?" Josh asked.

"You go down to where the park is, beyond the grand plaza? Then cross to the river's edge and take the bridge. It's a three-story building, built to be a school, but the ladies took it over. It's kind of a hospital."

"Hospital? That's a first," said Josh.

"They take care of people who need things done, you know, feed people, give out clothes, and minor first aid things. They're like a refuge, a place where people can stay if they are out on the street."

"So, they're being angels, then. Guardians. Are you saying they're reverting back to their former lives?"

"Kind of." Noel furrowed his brow. "But there's some public sentiment against what they're doing."

"Helping out?"

"They don't go to meetings," Spencer whispered. "That's their biggest offense."

Josh leaned back in the chair. "Why would someone care if they were helping people?"

Melanie spoke up. "Maybe it's not that they're helping. Maybe because it's their own plan and not coming from the committee? Could that be it?" she asked.

"Bingo," grinned Spencer again with a tinge of red still around his lips.

Josh had to ask. "Do you fellas go to meetings?"

They both nodded sheepishly. "Can't avoid it, not if you're going to be left alone."

"Why? What do you mean?"

"We heard a rumor the board is building a re-education camp, not a prison, but a place where they can put angels where they won't harm themselves or others," Spencer said.

"That just doesn't make any sense!" All this news was disturbing his belly. The joys of earlier in the day were not masking his growing fear. And he didn't care if Melanie felt it, because it involved her too.

"Spencer, where can we find out about this board? Do you have anyone you can trust he can talk to?" Melanie asked.

"I don't trust nobody. I just go to meetings and keep my mouth shut. I mean, doing this is risky enough for me."

"Name. Give me a name, fellas."

"The chairman's name is Francisco Kobyashi," said Noel. "He and his wife, Ping live in a huge red mansion overlooking the city. You can't miss it. But I wouldn't go there. That's probably the last place I'd go or take her. But you should know something. We were told Ping got up in the meeting the night before you arrived and asked everyone to find a way she could meet your Melanie. She already knew her by name."

"You knew this and didn't tell me?"

"We just found out about it not more than an hour ago," said Spencer.

"You know who you should talk to? That little guardian you turned, Annabel. She's the one who told us, and she seems to know a lot. I think she wants to help you, whatever it is you're doing." Noel added.

"We just saw her."

"My guess is, she's your best contact."

"And the guardians' house, would they accept visitors without being announced? Does that have to be arranged through her?"

"Well, I'm not sure they'd let you in without her," said Spencer. "She has lots of contact with those ladies and has even helped them. Helena's not too pleased, either. There's talk she might have to move there with them."

Spencer saw someone lurking in the distance. "Hey,

we gotta go, Noel. It's not safe to stay here too long and be seen. I'll try to stop by after my meeting with Kobyashi. You be careful. Go back to your quarters. Don't go walking around at night. Don't let anyone else in, either."

The two dark angels quickly scurried away, disappearing into the night air.

He had plans to perhaps take Melanie to a couple of his old haunts but now didn't feel safe doing so. They started back to their room.

He felt the presence of someone following him, so maneuvered back and forth through some of the older alleyways still untouched by the rebuilding program. These were places Joshua felt more in his element, and he knew some passageways that led between streets not many others knew about. They slipped into an open doorway leading to someone's apartment complex and waited several minutes in the shadows. A dark shadow passed by, pausing in the doorway and then disappearing into the alleyway.

Again, Josh felt like he'd been outmaneuvered by some secret hand. He weighed his choices. Part of him wanted to convince Melanie to leave tonight and return to the human world. That might buy them a day or two, but eventually he'd have to come back if he was going to keep his promise.

The logical choice, he determined, was not to react in fear or panic but to wait for Spencer's meeting update then go arrange for a private meeting with those former guardians and somehow enlist their help to return them up top. Sooner than later. But an event such as that would surely cause a stir. Any remaining guardians could be rounded up and hunted down.

He squeezed Melanie's hand. "Did you understand all of that?"

"I did. I'm very proud of you, Josh. I want to help."

She wouldn't look him in the eyes, but she pulled him close to the building's wall, telepathically asked him,

Is your apartment safe?

Chapter 10

M ELANIE WATCHED FOR the shadow that had been circling around, following them. She'd seen the same figure reflected in a store window earlier and pointed it out to Josh, who'd already known about it. He led them both through back streets, like a maze. They crisscrossed the old city. Luckily, not many were about. Everyone kept to themselves, almost like they were also escaping something haunting them.

Since their detour into the courtyard of someone's large home, the image swept by once and wasn't seen again.

She could read Joshua's tension and fear. He was doing a great job, however, of giving her specific thoughts of his worries, but she felt them burdening him. His face reflected his heightened awareness, but as they got closer to the little room, she noticed all the extra effort he was making to mask his emotions was taking a toll on him. He'd told her that he got little sleep the night before but hoped he could do so tonight.

Her former world of light and humanity had brought her such conflicting information, and it all was overwhelming to process. And, at first, this new adventure into the Underworld was everything she'd hoped, so completely different than she was used to. But Josh was the key. Without him, she was way out of her element and fear lurked at the edges like the being who followed them partway home. She recognized the signs of apprehension, her pulse quickened, and her stomach became cranky, even with her lack of appetite.

Still, their beautiful re-beginning, with the reunion she'd been dreaming about for years, and the rekindling of all the right things about Josh and their relationship were enough to keep her heart and soul burning for a future with him, no matter where it was and what it entailed. She could endure more of the unknown now, as if her new body gave her the additional strength to do so.

She waited from the shadows of a doorway while he opened the door, barely able to catch her breath, as she watched him fumble with the key card. The anticipation of being alone with him in private, in the tender candlelight of their playground made every cell in her body tingle. Maybe this heightened sense of danger and risk was what all dark angels experienced. Maybe this was to be how their life would flow. Connected to his thoughts, needing his touch, never wanting to leave his side, these were all things she'd never had before. This intensity between them only made her crave it even more. Was this a good thing, she wondered.

Am I changing? Is this the path I've chosen or something that will in time turn out to be a mistake?

She wanted to be part of Josh's solution, not his burden.

He motioned for her to cross the street and join him. Running into the dark, cold room, she looked for the switch to turn on their fireplace and stood by the hearth to feel the fire kick in to warm her chilled body.

Nearly safe, she'd begun to relax when she heard a scuffle at the doorway. Joshua was whispering something, but another voice, a woman's voice, laced with urgency, overpowered him. She saw a female hand reach out to block him from closing the door, and then she was inside while he locked the door behind them both.

It was Annabel, the former guardian Josh had turned.

Unlike humans seeking entrance into the Underworld, guardians only had to be caught having sex with a dark angel, and often that was what snagged them. Or that's what Claire, the only guardian Josh had lost, told her. Their wings would go black and their eyes would turn to nearly that same color. It didn't banish them to the Underworld forever, but Josh had told her they often were either ashamed or had accepted their life, the bed they'd made.

Melanie was surprised Annabel needed to see him. Checking her insides, she didn't yet feel any jealousy or animosity toward the petite former guardian, since the former guardian's turning and his claiming her happened before Melanie came into Joshua's life.

But again, that's what she'd been told. Not all of the story was known to her. Now would be a good time to sort them out once and for all.

The little guardian was smaller than Melanie by a few inches, more frail and slight of frame. She wore a dark cloak, covering her reddish-blonde hair that nearly matched the blaze from the fireplace. Josh turned on a table lamp, drew the only chair in the room for Annabel, and then took Melanie's hand as they both sat on the bed.

Let her speak her peace and then we'll ask her to leave.

She nodded her agreement.

Annabel was still cold, so scooted her seat closer to the fireplace. She clutched her cloak up to her neck.

"Thank you for agreeing to let me see you. It's getting so dangerous out there I had begun to give up hope. You do know, Joshua, you're safe here, right?" Her breathing was labored as she caught up to a normal rhythm, her eyes darting over the room, studying every detail.

"Because not everyone knows about it?" Joshua started. "But trust me, there have been others here. They brought Melanie to this place, so there are others who know."

"I realize that."

"Cass was Melanie's sponsor, and Naveen guided her. But as far as anyone else, who knows? And why do you say it's safe?"

"Before Mr. Kobyashi came to us, we had a director who used to keep a mortal woman here." Annabel examined her hands folded in her lap. "I-I can't be sure it was entirely voluntary."

"I hadn't heard that," Josh responded. "Go on."

"He had a protection device installed. I believe it works off the key, which you brought with you, I'm assuming—"

"I did."

"So, Cass must have the other one, then. You need to know that, first off. Perhaps you've already deduced it. But no one else can gain entry. There's an electrical current strong enough to vaporize anyone who merely breaks in without the key. The key gives permission."

"Until I change it."

"You could try. But who would do the work?"

"Never mind. Please, go on."

Annabel took a deep breath, and continued. "I want to start by saying trust no one."

"Okay, thanks for that information. I'm becoming more and more aware of that. Probably quicker to just retrieve my key from Cass, then."

"I would definitely do that tomorrow. It's a matter of safety. You know your way around here, but she—"

"I'm Melanie, you can call me that."

"Sorry." She spoke to Joshua. "Melanie is vulnerable without your protection, so if she stays here, she'll be safe, only as long as you alone have access, Joshua. Don't assume otherwise."

"Good point." Josh smiled at both the guardian and at Melanie. "If I could get her to stay in one place. Somehow I suspect she wants to be a part of everything I do. And perhaps that's how it should be."

Melanie felt the heat from his thigh burning hers. How she wanted to do something else right now. He heard her, and gently put his palm on her thigh, rubbing up and down gently. The reaction warmed her cravings and built her desire, in spite of all the danger.

"Suit yourself. But be careful," Annabel continued,

apparently oblivious to Josh's motions.

"We intend to. Go on."

"The story goes that the director, his name was Phillip something, wasn't here very long. He brought his girlfriend here, trying to convince her to turn. But he didn't survive the coup that started shortly after Mr. Kobyashi arrived. He was unseated and executed. Mr. Kobyashi executes his enemies. Not many people know this. But he's about to make it a regular spectacle, like the Roman arenas. They're building the place now."

Melanie's head was swimming with all this information. "What happened to the girl?" she asked.

"It is said Mr. Kobyashi and his wife share her bed, but no one's seen her for several months. It's whispered, though. People talk about her possible demise, her capture and possible torture. But no one really knows."

"Why would he do that?" She was curious to know.

"For compliance. They call themselves a collective, a rule by committee, but it's really rule by mob. He's caused a lot of fear amongst the population who've been here the longest. If you disagree, you are disappeared. He makes an example of you, or it's feared he has. This mortal woman, who obviously has been turned or killed, was made an example. No one can go against their reach. No one who knows how has lived to tell us all."

"I appreciate your warnings. But why tell me this about that director? Am I on some list of deplorables?" asked Josh.

"Not exactly. I think he would rather use you to help him consolidate his control. But if you resist, you need to know you're in danger. She is too." Annabel nodded to Melanie. "I'd have to add that she's in more danger than you, for reasons I just told you about."

Melanie's opinion of the little guardian was improving by the minute. She was risking her own life to tell them these things. But she had a question about it.

"Please, Annabel, why are you telling us this?" she asked.

"Because I want your help. Not everyone is in agreement with his policies and tactics. This feeling is deep below the surface and no one dares speak about it unless they are sure of the company. But most people here fear him. He's good at hiding his wrath, but once someone has crossed him, he goes ballistic. Scorched earth policy, and yes, before you ask me, he can vaporize."

"Damn," whispered Joshua.

"Did you get it back?"

"Get what back?" Melanie turned to Josh.

"Josh used to have the same skill—the vaporization

skill. Not everyone has it," Annabel reported without emotion.

"I haven't tried yet, but my hands feel sticky, which may mean I'm secreting something nasty, so perhaps it takes a while."

"If you have long enough, I hope in time it will come back. You're going to need it."

There was nothing worse than death by vaporization, she'd been told. Her former best friend and confident, Felix, had died a horrible, brutal death at the hands of Peter, the former director and his minions, who tried to kidnap Melanie and claim her for his own. He died violently, hovered over by the director's dark flying fire-breathing creatures with bat wings similar to what she studied at the clockmaker's studio. She felt sad for Felix. He'd been a pawn in a much bigger game and sacrificed his life to save her.

"Annabel, tell us the rest of it." Josh's voice now was calm and soothing, a long-practiced skill. Melanie knew he was masterful at getting information out of creatures, especially former guardians.

"So, like I said, not everyone is on board with these changes. At the same time, there are those who want to leave and feel they can't without great risk, and we need your help."

"You're talking about your former guardian sisters?

The ones who live in the big house?"

"Yes. But there are a few others too, not guardians but angels who have had enough. I've seen them at Helena's. I see it, because up until recently, I kind of moved under the radar. But now, things are getting dicey."

"I thank you for being brave to come here, and at some risk too. You could stay, if you would allow us to guest you," he said.

"Thanks but no. That would put me at greater danger if I don't return to Helena's. I know they are watching, Joshua. Someone would report me. Someone would do this to curry favor with someone. You see how it goes?"

Melanie squeezed his hand, moved by her statement and let him know how she felt. He responded by leaning in to her more, allowing more of his body to warm hers.

"Mr. Kobyashi knows it will look bad if everyone leaves en masse. Especially if key players or popular groups leave. Prominent members of the community have already left, or been disappeared, and that's what is so bad. We don't know who's managed to escape and who's been killed. But we are all certain he'd never willingly allow us to leave."

"Which leads to me, then. Is that what you're saying?"

"Yes. They want to talk to you, my former sisters do."

"That's perfect because I want to speak with them as well."

"But you must be very, very careful. And we don't feel as if we have much time. Some of these former guardians are not afraid to fight. Others are frozen in place, unable to function. Some think they should just get along and try to negotiate their way to a safer environment. Some have attended meetings, hoping to send the message they're willing to work with the committee. But we all know the longer it goes, the less likely we'll be able to leave, or live with the consequences of doing nothing."

"Completely understandable, Annabel. I think that happens with any group. At first, people are unhappy with things, but if the group is skillfully manipulated—and doing it by fear is effective but not always successful—soon those who would have stood up, no longer have a voice. They are trapped. I've tried to stay out of the politics of the Underworld for centuries for that very reason."

Melanie now understood more than ever why his devilish demeanor had won him so many conquests. He was the rebel figure, the odd warrior doing his silent thing. That made him not only the envy, but made him more powerful. And he also posed a threat to anyone trying to control the Underworld for their own personal gain. Josh was on a collision course with the director, or the committee he represented.

"And remember this, for your own sakes, you mustn't tell anyone you're going to meet with them. They want to set up a plan to escape. Josh, can you help us?"

Melanie saw the pride swelling in her lover's chest. But at the same time, she knew it would be easier to save themselves if they just bailed on the whole Underworld and went back home. She also knew that was wrong. She could see Joshua had no intention of deserting them.

"Then let's get this meeting settled, Annabel. Let's do it tomorrow. I'm to meet with Spencer, and then I can get over to the house."

"Good. Thank you. I was hoping you'd agree to help. I always knew you were a decent man, for a dark angel. Not all of the power you held over me was your glamour. I let myself fall because I wanted to." She dropped her eyes and blushed.

Melanie felt the reaction inside his heart, his care for the little guardian.

But all of a sudden, her internal alarm went off.

Here, just a few hours ago, she was thinking of opening up a florist's shop. How naive she had been. They *both* had been. The whole Underworld was an illusion, she noted. Nothing was what it seemed on the outside.

Annabel stood. "I'd better go." Josh rose to his feet as well.

"You're positive you don't want to stay?" Melanie asked. "Isn't it dangerous to be traveling now?"

"Thank you, Melanie. But no, my place is at Helena's with the other ladies, not here."

"Do you want to call me when it's arranged?" Josh offered.

"No, I don't have a phone. Besides, they aren't safe. With the right capability, you can be tracked with it."

"But I obtained it from the clockmaker."

"Do you think he would sacrifice his own station to help you? He'll help, but he wants something in return. He's also surrounded by Kobyashi's minions, who I'm sure spy on him. Slowly, one by one, all the good people, the people I trust, are being compromised. Soon there won't be anybody."

"Spencer and Noel, what about them?"

"Useful idiots, Josh. They're his ticket to seeking revenge on Audray and Jonas. I believe that is a long-range goal. Like yourself, they are legendary. Just your appearance around here has disrupted those who doubted the director could reach out upstairs and bring people back home. I know you need allies, but you should not tell them anything. Think about the position they are in. They bridge the gap between the Underworld and Jonas and Audray. Jonas' trust of them could be his undoing. And they go to meetings."

Josh sat back down, his face white as the sheets on their bed. Melanie could tell he was putting things together.

He'd been allowed to come back. They didn't *help* him. They helped Director Kobyashi bring him back, but they also helped bring Melanie back as well.

They could not be trusted, after all. His allies were pawns of the new enemy.

Chapter 11

JOSH HAD NEVER been close to feeling he was walking into a snowstorm larger than he was, so powerful that he had to consider whether or not it was worth taking this risk. But not for himself. He had Melanie to think about. What kind of a life would he have if he had immortality but no Melanie? And, as long as she was here with him in the Underworld, she would be his Achilles heel. It mattered little that he loved her or that she loved him. Anything that was worthy of being protected was his vulnerable spot. If he didn't understand this, he had no chance to find happiness or even how to design a future with her. With all the changes going on, the Underworld was now a much more dangerous place.

Perhaps he'd miscalculated all this. But, what choice did he have?

Joshua didn't like bullies. He preferred sweet-talking, effective people who might not be trustworthy, but that was the world he lived in, and he understood it. He wouldn't lead through fear and intimidation, even though he'd used some of that as he trained his recruits. He had some regrets there, especially the recruits who perished under his command.

He needed leaders who were full of themselves but still had enough courage to protect the innocent. Without allies like that, there was little chance Father's mission could be accomplished.

He'd always wondered why Father had watched him lose Melanie and languish in a world he didn't belong, and Joshua knew this was his wheel well.

His love for Melanie was the exact ploy this Kobyashi character needed to bring him down. Maybe Father used him as bait to wage another war at another time. Or maybe there was a flaw Joshua hadn't discovered yet.

He let the water sluice down his body as he showered alone. Josh wasn't sure, but he thought the sounds and the washing, healing waters would drown out some of his worry. He felt he had to carry the burden for both of them now. He had a big decision to make tonight. He wasn't looking forward to it, either.

The glass door opened as Melanie stepped in and stood at his backside, her arms wrapped around his chest, her cheek buried between his shoulder blades. His heart ached with the fullness of their love, their passion, her willingness to follow him anywhere, even if that was not in her best interest. Was she right to believe in him when he wasn't sure he had all the tools he needed to make this work?

God, how he wished things were different. Why had he thrown their relationship away like that? Why had he gotten so preoccupied with himself and his needs, been so shortsighted to think that just because he felt fat and had muscle aches for the first time that the human world was not worth living in? How could he have become bored with perfection? He'd had it all, and he tossed it aside like a hamburger wrapper. Threw away the beautiful, simpler life he would have had with her.

Wasn't it perfect that, just when everything was the most dangerous, she would come back into his life and never want to leave? Now? When he couldn't be assured of saving her.

Was the promise he'd made to Father too much? Could he be excused for taking her, running away, and just living somewhere on a beach where no one would find them?

Except he'd wake up every morning and think about the guardians like Annabel and the other ladies whose lives he'd forever altered.

Father must be laughing himself silly with the irony. Joshua Brandon, the legendary hunky dark angel hero of the Underworld had grown a conscience. And his penance was to work to free the women he'd ruined and perhaps sacrifice the one he wanted to inspire.

For the first time in his mortal or immortal life, he saw and felt both sides. Honor and justice became on par with his love and devotion for the woman he knew he was created to find, and to love and protect forever. Because if he didn't do this, he couldn't have her either. She'd know that, eventually, something else would come up and be more prominent in his life and he'd be faced with another choice. She could never really be sure of him, because he wasn't sure of himself.

"Don't torture yourself, Joshua," she whispered to his back, kissing him. She'd read his thoughts, so he pulled up a mental shield to block her discovery.

He bent his head down and allowed the water to completely refresh his thoughts. *How much has she learned?*

If she heard him, she didn't show it. Her hands brushed down the fronts of his thighs, meeting in the center, gently fondling him as she pressed her breasts into his back. Her gentle moan echoed throughout the small shower, enhanced by the ache in his own heart. He wished she didn't love him so deeply. It would be much better for her if....

I have to stop you, my love. This is nonsense.

Her soft message caused him to tense his abdomen. He inhaled abruptly when her hands rubbed the cavern above the muscles of his lower torso, then smoothed over his chest, pinching his nipples. Her wetness and desire gave off the heady aroma he could live off of. He could stay in her arms all day, all night and never want for anything. He wished that was a realistic option for them.

He turned to face her. His erection told her some of what he had to say, but not all. She was Father's miracle of creation. He was standing in his shower, aroused, just before all Hell was about to break loose. They called it gallows humor, and he'd heard the stories of condemned prisoners giving each other a little time of pleasure before all was taken away. He understood it in its very blackest sense. It was, in effect, an act of redemption. A triumph over fear. The indignity and degradation of death could hold no sway for beings created to come together and heal each other. Nothing was more noble. And in that way, they cheated their despicable circumstances. They cheated death itself.

Give me your pain, your fear, Joshua. Use me to excise those demons. Let me take some of this away from you. Can you? Can you let me take this burden from you?

Her beautiful face glowed as she looked up to him with her full lips lusciously craving him. Her thighs demanded his touch and caress. Her breasts begged to be suckled. Her sex required violation in the most loving and beautiful way. He needed to push hard, to crawl inside her warm love for him and let it flow all over him, so he could shed this skin and rise up whole, ready for battle. It was so wrong she was here with him, but it was also so right. He knew, flawed as he was, that he was the only being in the universe who could save her.

He knelt before her, pressing his forehead against her belly, a belly she'd wanted to fill with children like Audray and Jonas had. He wanted to make her burst with his seed, so he'd be impossible to forget. So something of his would remain forever.

His fingers rubbed against that soft place below her belly button, feeling the vacant cavern there. His lineage should live on. He might not be able to win the battle, but he could conjur the magic of their love, turn it into a physical being, sweet-talk it and prolong its stay. He wanted to see a part of them develop and grow, unlike anything in the Underworld. This place of death and endless forevers.

His fingers slipped below to her warm quivering sex as he looked up at her staring back down on him. She let him feel the passion rising, the threshold of desire as he breached her flesh and stroked her insides with all the tenderness he could find.

I don't deserve—

She cut him off, wouldn't let the thought finish. Her fingers covered his mouth and then his ears. She pushed his head lower, his mouth and tongue at her entrance she spread for him as she arched back into the tiled walls of the shower.

If you don't taste me now, I will explode.

Yesssss. And yesssss. He focused on the soft folds of her velvet petals, his tongue thirsty for her, stroking her bud. His lips sucked it firm and stiff before he let it slip through his teeth, making her jump and then moan her pleasure. Her fingers rubbed his head, massaging the top of his spine and slipping around the back of his ears. She matched the rhythm of his feeding on her with the tips of her fingers bringing him peace, comfort, love, possibility.

He rose up, understanding that he was the man who she'd chosen, the only man in the universe who could rock her world. The golden mantle of her love for him he wore like a crown. He was twice the being he was before just because she believed in him.

He wrapped his arms around her, lifted her from the shower, and carried her soaking wet to the bed. Steam arose from her body, glistening in the light of the fire. Her limbs were like rubber. Her arms held him, loved him, her fingers found their little special places as he kissed her from her neck to her belly button. He pushed her breasts up with the palms of his hands and then squeezed, ending with a nipple pinching and a soft kiss.

"Melanie, Melanie," he whispered to her open mouth. Her lips and tongue drew him in. His pelvis moved against hers. Her response was to be the cradle he rocked in, matching him, feeling his member pressing, begging entry, rubbing against her mound, and demonstrating his hardness and his ardor.

She raised her right leg, bent at the knee. His hand smoothed her wet flesh from the back of her knee to where her womanhood pulsed. He slid his arms beneath her, holding her shoulders and pulling her down as he arched up and filled her with that exquisite joining.

He stopped to study her face as it registered her passion. She was open, willing. He knew she'd even die for him. Her eyes were half lidded, her chest blotchy red and heaving. Inch by inch he came inside, all the while they watched each other and the miracle of how it felt to be so connected with someone he never wanted to leave.

It is like that, Josh.

Always will be, Melanie.

Nothing can stop this. Our lovemaking is a practice, an ongoing story of more.

Yes, more.

He knew he'd remember this night for all eternity or for however much time he had. He felt her probing his thoughts, but not intruding. Like the lovemaking, their performance combined their physicality with being deep inside each other's thoughts. Her messages made him harder, made him feel more of a man than he ever had. He told her of her beauty. He begged her to release, to ride that wave he was creating and show him her peak.

I'll give you everything, my love.

He studied her, as if he had to remember forever how it was to truly love a woman, to put himself inside someone whom he desired more than life itself.

Take me with you, sweet Melanie.

And so, she did.

Chapter 12

S HE AWOKE IN the early morning hours, hearing the sounds of water. She wondered if, somehow, they could hear rain in this little apartment.

But as she fully focused and her mind cleared, she realized it was the sound of the shower that they'd forgotten to turn off. It had run all night long.

She kissed his forehead, sliding out from under him carefully, trying not to wake him.

Tiptoeing toward the bathroom, she switched off the water at last. She wasn't sure how it worked in the Underworld, but at home, she'd have a hundred-dollar bill for that transgression.

Coming back into the room, she drank in the form of her lover, his naked buttocks glowing in the firelight, his hair in baby ringlets at the sides of his cheeks and covering his forehead and eyes. He had one knee bent. His hands clutched the pillow he slept on. She was grateful he'd gotten some rest at last.

She gently tucked the sheet over him and then returned to bed, but he awoke.

"Everything okay?" he asked in a whisper.

"We left the shower running. All night long."

"Uh oh. I guess the water police will be after us. Hurry, let's run!" He grabbed her, tickling her until she told him to stop. By the time he quit, nearly all the sheets and pillows were on the floor.

"I wasn't done sleeping, Josh. That's not fair."

"Then you shouldn't have awakened me." He proceeded to pick up the pillows and straighten the sheets. She helped him in silence.

She'd discovered her need for food was practically nil, but when he asked her if she wanted to go out, she wasn't sure how to answer truthfully.

"I'm not really hungry. Besides, is it safe?"

He shrugged and sat on the edge of the bed, his legs crossed at the ankles, naked. His tanned and perfect body was toned, showing off more muscle mass than he'd had before their separation. But his physical strength appeared to be growing, as was hers.

"What's got you so pensive, Josh?" She started putting on the clothes Cass had allowed her to take from the center's closet.

He too started to dress. After watching him pull a knitted shirt over his head, smoothing it down over his flat abdomen, she was ready to ask him to take it off.

He pretended to start to do so, which sent her eyebrows up into her hairline. But then he dropped his hands, his shoulders, and stretched out his arms. "Come here, Melanie."

She snuggled against him, loving the scent of their lovemaking still present. She took in a deep breath, exhaled, and whispered, "Promise me you won't ever shower again. I like the way you smell."

"That's something I *do* understand. This—this heightened sense of smell and taste—I missed this up there." He sat on the edge of the bed and asked her to sit across his lap.

She was going to probe what was on his mind but stopped before she got very deep, respecting his request of last night.

He kissed the side of her cheek. "We have to talk about something I was going to bring up last night, but…"

The closeness to him, the effect of his breath on her neck and her cheek, and the rumble of his voice in her ear set her floating somewhere else. She loved the way she felt, the memories of all the things they did last night still bright and fresh in her mind.

"Yes, I'm seeing those images too, Melanie. I'm going to be doing so all day, I'm afraid." He nuzzled her ear before kissing her neck right below as she bent her head away, giving him access. "I'm completely going to be driven insane by you, but what a way to go, huh?" he said before they kissed. Then through their nibbles, he added, "And while this is lovely, it does present some problems we have to discuss."

She pulled her head back to search his face.

"What are we talking about, Josh?"

"Honey, I went over it so many times last night, tried to look at things from as many different angles as possible, and I've come to the conclusion you're going to have to go back to Jonas and Audray's for a bit until I finish here."

She stood, suddenly fearful of his next words.

"When did you come to this conclusion?"

"There's no way out. Surely you can see that, honey?"

"No, Josh. I see it completely differently. I'm in it all the way."

"But I think if you truly understood what could happen…I mean, Annabel was right. You're in even more danger than I am. And that's what I'm worried about. They'll use you to get to me, like they already did. They'll do it again."

"But how can I do this? First, how will I get successfully back to the human world?"

"I was going to ask Annabel today when I saw her."

154

"You can't be serious, Josh. You don't even know any of those guardians will help you, and you already were warned about Spencer and Noel. And let me add, you had no idea they might be working against you. That's where all that dark angel intuition was getting you. I think I was more suspect of them than you were."

He'd started listening with his head hung, watching the ground, nodding. It made her angry to be speaking to the top of his head, and she feared he was tuning her out, not even listening.

She crouched in front of him. Taking his hands in hers, she angled down until she made eye contact. "Josh, this is me talking. I'm not going to abandon you now. I can't do that. You need me. Don't you see that?"

He didn't want to look her in the eyes. Her heart sank as she realized he'd already made up his mind. She feared there would be no way convincing him otherwise.

"I'm going to be honest with you, sweetheart," he said as he drew her palm to his mouth and tenderly kissed her. "You'd be in my way. You'd compromise what I have to do. And there's a lot at stake."

"No—" She tried to pull herself up, but he held her hands down, close to his chest.

"Yes, Melanie. It's the only way. I can't let you fall

into harm's way. I have to get you out of here. Now, as a compromise, I'll agree to take you back myself, but I'm telling you the truth to say it will make my work here more difficult. Will signal more of a shift. And there is the possibility they'd stop me. Stop us. Capture us, Melanie."

"They already know."

"We aren't sure. I'm looking for the best chance of your survival."

"What about your survival, Josh? I can't live without you."

"Not as important. But you are. If I don't release those guardians and break the back of this directorship, there is no chance. And, I fear this director's quest for power goes beyond this world. So if I fail here, no one is safe. Maybe it wouldn't happen right away, but in time, they'd all come after all of you anyway."

"And you'd be gone. No one left to defend us, if you could spare me being totally selfish. But it's true. Jonas and the others would fight, but what can they do against—"

"You might have another ally. You might have Father."

"What? So he can transform me to a guardian? Live forever without you? Go through their wash so I'm forever wiped of our happy memories. I don't want that." She got back on her knees again. "I want to be by your side, fighting right alongside you. If you go down, I want to go down there with you. Give me that honor, please."

"They're smarter than that, Melanie. We'd be separated like that." He clicked his fingers. "It would be easy. They'd hold it over me, Melanie. Do you want me to live a life of doing despicable things, watching me become a shell of what I could have been, just so they don't harm you? And they'd harm you anyway. Those scars wouldn't heal. Even if we got away, think of the other innocent loss of life. You want all that on your conscience?"

He was a silver-tongued bastard who could make a concrete column have an orgasm. She was fighting him but with both her hands and her feet bound. It was so unfair.

"Let's first go see the guardians together. Then, if you still feel that way, I'll leave voluntarily, Joshua. Can we negotiate that?"

She had hope because a sexy one-sided smile erupted on his lips. His eyes were soft, his tongue licked his lips. He held her head in his hands and gave her a deep kiss so hot it felt like her clothes were going to catch fire.

"I'd rather just stay here with you all day in bed.

We could make love until they found some way to get in here. They already have a key, but we could do that.... love away the hours, steal whatever future we could have for just a little bit longer, holding each other because we knew it was all going to end. We could do that, and it would be more effective than you going with me."

She began to cry, completely let down from everything she'd been hoping for.

"That's what it would be doing, Melanie. If I walk out there with you, it would be like me handing you over to them. All would be lost, my love. That would be the act that could erase not only us but everyone. Everyone we care about."

She didn't want to hear it. He pulled her head into his chest, held her while she cried into his shoulder. He stroked the back of her head as she sobbed.

"I know it's not what you want to hear, but we need to be in combat mode. We have to fight. But it's my fight, something I have to do alone. And you have to be strong and vigilant up top. You'll help warn and protect Audray and Jonas. Their children. Think of their children, Melanie."

She finally pulled away and wrestled to her feet.

"Oh stop! Why don't you just tell me you don't want me anymore? That would be so much easier."

"But that would be a lie. I do this because I need you to be safe. If I know you're safe, that gives me reason, power. It brings me the energy to do what I need to do. Surely you see that, sweetheart?"

She wiped the tears from her cheeks. Today she'd had so many plans. She wanted to become his secret weapon against the evil growing. She didn't want to run away. She wanted to stand and fight. Right next to him as a full partner.

He came to his feet and approached her, but she backed up.

"Fair enough. I get it, Melanie. Now, what I'm going to do is find Annabel, and I'll send her here. So, you'll wait here for her, where you're safe. You let no one else in, understand? The two of you will not be missed for a time. That will give me a chance to get my plans put together. And I'll start executing them once I know you're safe."

"How will we get out?"

"The back way. The way you came in. She'll bring a lantern, and the two of you will make your way out. You do remember where you opened the portal door, don't you?"

"Yes."

"Then you can lead her back to the Starlings. You tell Jonas everything, you hear?"

Slowly, with her heart breaking, she nodded. And then she broke the standoff and threw herself into his arms again. "Promise me. Promise me you'll come back."

"I did before, remember? I promise, Melanie, no matter what. I will find you and bring you back to be with me, either in this world or the one upstairs. But I promise you we'll be together forever, sweetheart."

Chapter 13

IT WAS HARD to say good-bye to Melanie, because he couldn't show her how broken he felt inside at the prospect of possibly never seeing her again. She had not stopped crying ever since he leveled with her about his thoughts. By convincing her, he was, in effect, convincing himself too. He could live with a failure for a mission. He couldn't live with failure and lose her too.

The longer he stayed said his farewells, the more she'd doubt his confidence. It was important that she thought he was concretely certain this was the right plan and that it would work out, because he knew all the players and the lay of the land so well.

But just the opposite was the case.

In the end, he acted annoyed with her tears, lectured her about getting a grip and putting on her big girl panties, and all that crap when all he wanted to do was tell her she'd given him the gift of life in her love for him, and if he was lucky, he would be forever grateful. He'd spend the rest of his days making up to her those lost years when they were separated.

But of course, he couldn't say any of that.

"You're scaring me, Melanie. You don't think I can do this. Is that what you're saying?"

"No, Josh. I just don't want you to go."

And then the tears would come and he'd have to wait another five minutes before she could talk again.

So, he'd finally said it. "Dammit, Melanie. I have to keep my wits about me. Have a little faith. Don't jinx it with your negative attitude. I wouldn't do this unless I knew this was the way. I'm the one who is headed for battle. You'll be back in the human world. Safeguarded by men who would do anything to protect you. You're going to have to get much tougher than you're demonstrating. I need you to believe in me. Pull yourself together, or I'll feel it, and it will throw me off. You could actually do me harm. That's why you have to go home."

She cried at that. He understood completely how she felt but couldn't say it.

She tried so hard to kiss him without her eyes and forehead wrinkling, her lips turning down into a frown. She bravely hugged him. "Only good, positive thoughts. That's all I have."

She briefly turned and wiped her cheeks and then

presented herself back to him with the smile he'd been looking for. And he told her so.

He'd remember that look of hers forever. Her face was why he was fighting, worth all the risk he was going to take.

Just before he slipped out the door, he whispered, "If she's not back here in two hours, you go. Go by yourself."

She'd started to react, but he held his hand up, begging to stop the objection.

"It won't happen, Melanie, but if it does, that's what you do. See if you can find some candles you could use to find your way out and go back home. I'll join you soon. Very soon."

That last kiss nearly did him in, feeling the way she shook, trying so desperately to look brave for him. He loved her even more for that.

Without any further hesitation, he was out the door and halfway down the alleyway before he looked behind him to make sure the coast was clear, and it was. He didn't see anyone nearby.

But now this waiting for Spencer to show up was proving difficult. His eyes burned. He thought perhaps it was the slightly acid smell in the air. It wasn't going to be sunny today. Joshua masked his emotions, hoping to give himself enough cover to get away with the planned escape for Melanie and Annabel. He considered that perhaps the angel's meeting with Francisco Kobyashi had complications.

He had more than a couple of things he needed to keep secret. He couldn't let on that he no longer trusted Jonas' two dark angel former colleagues. He needed to make casual his communications with Annabel and try to convince the angel he was being summoned to the guardianship house but didn't really want to attend and might not show up.

And he needed information about the gentleman, the Underworld's former director, who had stayed in his room and what became of the human woman he sheltered there, but only if it was safe to do so. That was because the only possible source for that information was Annabel unless he could make up another way he could have been told about it.

He'd figure something out, he told himself.

He was early, which probably wasn't the brightest idea, but he was nervous biding his time. Josh wanted to give his body distance from Melanie, give himself the opportunity to recover what he could control of his thoughts. He also needed to find Annabel, who was supposed to meet him in the courtyard, except now he considered that risky. When they were speaking last night, he didn't pick up that either of the angels had the gift of telepathy, which was something going in his favor.

His only saving grace was that Annabel didn't trust the two darks either. So perhaps she'd have the wits to avoid coming into the picture with them present.

He was keen on obtaining any more information he could about Kobyashi himself, with hopes he'd a weak spot. The directorate knew Joshua's weakness. He needed something on the other side to shore up his defenses.

Groups of two or three individuals scurried by without taking any notice of him. The air was chilly, not yet warming up to the day, but it was going to be a gray day anyway. He had neglected to bring a jacket, so he was cold.

From behind, someone had approached, and before he could react further, his head up to his ears was sandwiched between two enormous breasts. Her perfume was hard to miss as well.

Helena.

He stood for the legendary Madame of the foremost house in the Underworld. She had all the best girls, many of them he'd escorted there himself. She was a valuable ally during his time there because she knew so many things about so many people.

"You are as lovely as I remember, sweetheart." He

was overplaying, but until he knew which side of the fence she fell, it was safer that way.

She wore all red, which was the fashion all over the Underworld. Her classic bustier shoved her cleavage nearly to her neck, her womanly wares on full display like candy treats to a starving population. It was all as it was intended to be. He made sure to show her he was not afraid to look at her and admire her essence or reveal how it affected him. Whatever playacting she had done with him, he always answered back with even more intensity. Then neither one of them had to have hurt feelings in the end. It left their relationship clean, strictly for sex, but hinting that it was much, much more.

He knew what that was now.

"You are a devil still, aren't you? Your woman hasn't bridled you I see."

He held his arms out to the sides. "As you can see, I'm alone, not quite as available as I look, but she trusts me to have my business dealings outside of her knowledge."

She leaned into him so deeply that the tips of her nipples, nearly bursting out of her bodice, barely grazed his sweater. He held his breath for what was to come next.

"You find that very wise, Joshua? Trusting you?"

Her dark eyes sparkled, the small garnet earrings glinting from the reflection of light coming from somewhere.

"Am I not trustworthy, Helena? I deliver what I promise, as do you, my dear. Every single time. You have for centuries."

She studied him before answering. "You gave it all up, I hear. Why would you come back? You were free."

"Careful, I might accuse you of being jealous, or is it that white dress and a veil you secretly dream about, Helena, all virginal, the blushing bride, taking kids to school and cleaning the house? You don't have difficulty seeing how I might find that lifestyle boring?"

"I would think it would depend on what she did for you in the bedroom. For some, you might not be able to walk afterwards, or so I've been told."

"That's usually what they tell me, sweetheart."

"So it was a fantasy living as a human, just an ordinary man and not the great and powerful dark angel who made Father's angels want to touch themselves in forbidden places?"

He'd always loved how all the right words, flattery and challenge hinted at the prospect of something so much steamier right around the corner if one took advantage of it. Her subtlety and skill took his breath away.

They could have made a formidable pair if that had been what he wanted. But although he'd bedded her hundreds of times and loved every encounter, she didn't make him cry when he had to leave her in the morning. And he wouldn't consider giving up his life, either immortal or human to keep her safe. That warm spot was already taken, and it was a pity. He grieved for something that never could have been. But it was a pleasant thought.

"What is it you fantasize about, my sweet?"

She let her guard down for just a second, and that told him everything. "I don't kneel for someone's whim. I'll kneel to take a man into my mouth and make him lose his mind. I'll kneel to play the part of a girl being taken for the first time if that's required. I'll kneel to take care of one of my girls who has been beaten and vow revenge and…"

He detected a red flash of anger there, a speck of resentment, a thick drop of it so powerful it would turn a swimming pool blood red with just one. "Go on, I'm listening."

"I'd kneel to the man who could not only liberate that part of me that releases during intercourse but that part of me that worries for the future of my ladies. That I could count that they'd come back safe and uninjured and have a future that isn't filled with pain."

To the casual observer, it would appear that she had made a sexual pass at him, and he had accepted. His fingers touched her cheek as he bent and kissed her without opening to her. Then he quickly embraced her, whispering in her ear, "Are you not safe, Helena? Are they demanding something more than sex?"

She stood on tiptoes, pretending to press herself into him, alluring him to come visit her again, as someone who knew them might think. But instead, she whispered, "Obedience. They are demanding obedience."

The part about going to Helena's that Josh had always loved was that it was a given her ladies were there for one thing and one thing only: To give pleasure. But it was never demanded. It was always freely given with all the abandon she or any of her other ladies could give. Demanding obedience from someone so giving was, in Joshua's mind, unforgivable.

Many women Josh had known in the human world wouldn't understand that Helena could freely give up her body but not her loyalty. That was something that couldn't be bartered for and must not be taken.

"If I come asking for Annabel, will you be jealous?"

"No, just as long as you take me the next time."

"I was worried for her safety last night—"

"She came home intact and of good cheer, Joshua. You did indeed bring me an angel, my love. I love her like a daughter."

"Then let it be, Madame. Have her come to my rooms as soon as she can. Tell her someone awaits her arrival, then. Or can you not promise this?"

"On my life, I can. And may I have yours?"

"Which is?" he whispered, separating them at last.

"No harm will come to her."

"On my life." He touched her cheek again.

She backed up, still holding on to his hand, and then they released each other. She was gone in mere seconds.

He sat down and continued to wait for Spencer, struck by the changes he'd witnessed. He'd seen a madame become a mom to a motherless angel and seek for something more precious than love. Both the women were striving to make a better life. That was not an Underworld trait.

No wonder Kobyashi was worried.

ABOUT THE TIME Joshua realized he'd been set up and Spencer wasn't going to show, he saw the dark angel emerge from the platform that took the tram up to the government buildings. He had someone with him he didn't recognize.

Spencer was laughing, nodding his head and being more animated than he was used to seeing. Joshua deduced why.

The man next to him matched the pictures around the Underworld of Director Francisco Kobyashi. He wasn't tall, but rather stocky and appeared to have one hip that gave him a limp. His clothes were plain but pressed perfectly. His face showed he wore makeup, even lipstick.

"Joshua! So sorry I'm late. I have a real treat for you. This is Francisco Kobyashi, the director himself. When I told him I was meeting with you, he insisted on coming."

Spencer's animated tone wasn't fooling Josh at all, and he knew it but continued to play Kobyashi's pet dog.

"Mr. Brandon. I have heard so much about you," he said as he held out his hand for a shake.

The man was a clean slate. Incredibly proper, he even afforded Joshua a bow.

Joshua shook his hand, endured the over-the-top squeeze in that passive aggressive manner when two men were having a pissing match. He did not play along.

"I am so pleased to meet you. I too have heard much about you," he said to Kobyashi as he quickly removed his hand from the vice grip of their shake and bowed afterward, slightly lower than had been given him. Kobyashi's eyes widened in unexpected curiosity.

"But where is your lovely better half, Joshua? I've heard she's so beautiful. You must bring her by our home. We'd like to entertain you sometime soon."

"How about tomorrow night, sir?" Joshua said quickly before he could think of anything else he wasn't supposed to reveal.

"Perfect. Spencer here can tell you how to get there, won't you?"

"I'd be delighted to join you all," said Spencer.

"No, I didn't invite you. I invited him and his lovely lady, Melanie. But you will please see to it that they will be at my house tomorrow night at seven?"

Spencer frowned but agreed.

"Well, I wanted to meet you. I have an appointment to rush off to across town, and I'm afraid I'll be late. But I couldn't pass up the chance to welcome you here personally. I hope we'll be working well together in the coming days."

"I'd love to hear about it, sir."

"I have some pet projects I'd like to discuss."

"Absolutely. You've done an amazing job here with all these new buildings, the improvements you've made. It's quite impressive. I'd love to be a part of it."

"Thank you. I have big plans." He winked at Josh, a little too long for Josh's comfort, and then ran quickly in the opposite direction.

"Wow," Joshua said to Spencer as they both took

chairs. "He's intense. But he's methodical, knows exactly what he wants." He followed the director's body as it got smaller and smaller and then disappeared completely.

"He seems to have taken to you. Around here, that's either a good thing or a bad thing. I think in your case it's good."

"I'm glad you think so." Joshua chose his words carefully. "How did your meeting go?"

"Kinda hard to tell. He showed me his plans for the welcome center. He's asked me to consider working for him, recruiting angels, especially guardians, both here and up top, to come join us."

"You mean turn them?"

"Well, the earthly guardians, yes. But he'd like the guardians you brought here to get more involved with his programs. The strength of his systems is that everyone works together, everyone does their part. There are some here that think they can just exist, or that they were created to work as an individual rather than a collective. That creates certain inequities if not everyone participates. He'd like the guardians to take a more active role."

"I see."

"It's really not much. I'm sure they'll come around."

"I think you're right. Then it doesn't fall on just a

few people's shoulders. And it's easier to manage that way." Josh was giving points he suspected had been given to him and wasn't displeased when Spencer agreed with all of them.

"So, did you talk to Annabel?" Spencer asked, without making eye contact.

"I was rather hoping she'd stop by here. She knew the two of us were going to meet."

"She might have come by, but not when Kobyashi was present."

"Why do you say that?"

"He's been reminding her to be a good example for the ladies at Helena's."

"I see. So, where's Noel?"

Spencer chuckled. "He's got himself a hot date. He'll tell me tomorrow he's in love. He does that every time."

"What happens? Why so many false starts?"

Spencer leaned forward on the table. "Well, I shouldn't be telling you this, but he had a gal up top. He didn't know she was still alive. So, on one of his visits, he ran into her. He goes to see her any chance he gets. I had to cover for him with Kobyashi, but that's where he is."

"So he's trying to bring her here?"

"Ideally. It's a hard sell. He doesn't have your talents, Josh."

"Isn't there someplace she could come, like my apartment, where she could check it out for a weekend or something? Maybe she could be convinced that way. Explain to her the lack of aging, all that. In my experience that's what gets them. Offer them something no one else has."

Josh hoped he'd pick up the bait but wasn't so lucky. Apparently Spencer didn't know very much about the former occupant of his apartment or the former director.

"I'll mention it. He's due back tomorrow. We'll have to go shopping and get you some decent duds. Ping likes men who are well put together. We'll get you something professional, make you look irresistible." He leaned in closer and whispered. "And we'll make you smell nice. The ladies love it. But especially Ping. She's a connoisseur of handsome men and, Joshua, you're exactly her type. Trust me."

Joshua chuckled, attempting to act casual.

"Just to be clear, I'm to be irresistible to Ping for what reason?" he asked.

"For your advancement."

"But they run a collective. Doesn't that mean—"

"Oh, Josh, that applies to all the little people. You and I? We have more important jobs, and we're looked up to. And, trust me, things will go a lot better if Ping likes you."

Chapter 14

MELANIE OPENED JOSH'S front door when she heard the soft knock, guessing it was Annabel. The young angel burst in, closing the door herself behind her.

"Oh, God! Free at last!" Her cheeks were flushed, and she gulped a deep breath.

"You were followed?" Melanie asked.

"I'm sure of it, but I've gotten good at eluding them. The director sends people to watch after me all the time."

"And that is why?"

"I spend more time at the Guardian House than at his meetings. The man is fixated on me. I feel more like a bug with a pin stuck through her."

Melanie slowly addressed a question that arose. "Are you—are you having sex with him?"

"Oh, God no. Not sure what he's into, but it isn't straight sex. I've not been to parties at their home, but some of the girls have. He creeps me out." She handed

Melanie a cloak similar to hers. "We make these at the house. It works to disguise us when we have to travel at night."

Melanie took the deep burgundy cape with hood. She noted the hand-sewn seams, all lovingly over-stitched in embroidery thread so that no rough edges showed anywhere. On the front of the cape was a symbol hand stitched in tiny gold thread. It looked like an anchor with wings.

"What's this symbol?"

"It's our internal symbol of the resistance here." She pulled her skirts up and showed the same symbol tattooed to the inside of her ankle on her right. "This means you can trust the one who wears it, unless you are part of the directorate, that is."

"I wish Josh knew this. Where did you get the symbol from?"

"It's an ancient Christian symbol, actually, since before the Roman times. When Christians and Jews were one people. The anchor is for being a fisher of the human soul, the wings are meant for the angelic horde, and originally this circle at the top was to symbolize the Creator. We've just adopted it as a method to stay united."

"But when you wear this cloak, aren't you giving away who you are?"

"No, because that's the house symbol. But I'll grant you, it's one of the things Kobyashi doesn't like. He has his own symbols—pagan sun symbol variations. There would never be a cross on anything he produces."

"Nor would I have ever expected it here in the Underworld."

"The cross symbol is one of sacrifice. That's a guardian thing. That's what we used to do. But underworld dark angels have been doing battle for eons, Melanie, mostly warring amongst themselves. Not all of them were bad. There's a long mythology I'll tell you about someday if you're interested."

"You're talking about *dark angel light*, aren't you? The sugar-free version? The diet version?" Melanie asked, meaning it halfway as a joke. It calmed her nerves to think of it that way. Josh wasn't an evil being. He'd seen the "light" as they say. He could never be a pure dark angel again. It wasn't in his DNA.

Annabel nodded. "Perceptive. I think I like that assessment. Makes it easier to understand why some of us are more conflicted than others." She scanned the room. "Everything ready to go? Are you bringing anything?"

"I found this satchel in the closet. I'll take a few things, but I haven't much." She showed the black bag, stuffed with all the colorful tops she could fit.

"Then we're off. That is what we're doing, right? Going back to the human world? You know the way?"

"Yes. Did you bring a flashlight? It's pitch dark, and dirty."

She held up the lantern. "Helena told me to. I just need to light it, and it should burn for several hours. How long will it take?"

"Close to an hour."

Annabel used a sliver of kindling she found by the hearth, ignited it, and lit her glass lantern. Melanie checked to make sure the door was locked, left the fireplace on, and turned off lights. She withdrew heavy drapes covering the back wall, revealing the doorway she'd entered through with Naveen. The thought of going back to the dark tunnel made her shiver, but it was what she'd agreed to do, what Josh was counting on. And she was taking a very important package with her, Annabel.

She opened the doorway, her face getting blasted with a cold metallic-smelling wind that seemed to groan at their discovery. She ushered Annabel out with the lantern, scanned the room one more time, inhaled, swung the drapes over the door opening, stepped out into the tunnel, and slammed the door shut. Under the light of the lantern, she verified the latch was securely closed. The face of the beast illuminated in the golden glow seemed to snarl at her.

"No way back now. We go this way," she whispered to Annabel, directing her to go to the right. "Keep to the wall. Do you want me to go first?"

"Yes, please. Look at this place. I don't like it, Melanie. What's in here?" she said as she raised the lantern above her head to give the area light. "Are those tracks?"

"Yes, but you see, they are walled off down there. I guess they used to go into the Underworld."

"Like the other transport stations," said Annabel. "Wonder why this portal was closed?"

"I have no clue." Melanie instructed her to hold the lamp up over her shoulder so she could see the path.

Just like before, the chill hit her all the way to her bones. Debris of all sorts littered the tracks and the platform on the other side. She could also see broken windows no longer protecting dark rooms that looked abandoned. There were more wooden shipping boxes with what appeared to be rags but could have been clothing at one time. Broken chairs, bent wheels, and an odd assortment of metal chains lay at the side.

"This place is pure evil, Melanie."

"No kidding. But it's so much better to see with the light. When I came through, I couldn't even see my hand in front of my face. It was that bad."

S. HAMIL / SHARON HAMILTON

They heard a sound in front of them. Annabel threw her cloak over the lamp to dim the light, and the two women waited in the dark, pressed against the stone walls of the tunnel. Melanie felt the moisture from the old stones, and as she rubbed her fingers, she could feel a fine grit. Down at her feet she had stepped part way on something metal. She bent over and felt the length of it, determined it was a short piece of pipe.

"What is it?" Annabel asked.

"I've found a weapon, I think."

They remained still, listening for further sounds, but after several seconds, they continued. Just as Annabel was bringing out the lantern from under her cloak, they heard the unmistakable flapping of a large bird.

"Oh God, one of those things. I hope they aren't living here."

"What things?" Melanie asked.

"They eradicated most of them, but every once in a while, we find pockets of the creatures who got away. They had been doing experimentation on old beings during another directorship. They are afraid of fire, but if you see red eyes, that means they are fully capable of the fire breathing. Deadly."

"Shhh. Let's listen."

The flapping noise had distanced, and with nothing

181

else except the moaning wind whirling through the tunnel, they continued.

Melanie stepped over a long-dead bird that had nearly turned to dust. A wooden crate with glass bottles in it, all with their tops smashed, was upended on the tracks to their left. Some sort of syrupy mixture had leaked over the crate and the ground and smelled putrid. Several dead animals lay nearby which looked like varieties of opossum. Their skeletons curved, limbs curled up toward their bodies, and their teeth barred, as if they died a horrible death.

After several minutes, there was less debris, and Melanie was relieved they didn't run across any more lifeless creatures. They passed an alcove in the stone wall. An old sleeping bag and mattress lay torn with dirty stuffing collecting dark waters seeping from the walls.

Across the tracks was a landing area, with a ramp that led down to another level. At the top was a large rack made of metal piping forming a square, upturned U-shape. Hanging from the rack were chains of various sizes. But as they got closer, both women noticed the chains were dripping in some bloody excrement and feces. The stench was strong enough to make Melanie gag.

"It was a creature, Melanie. They perch, like birds

do. And since they only eat meat, their stools are always bloody like that."

"So, they're here after all?" she asked, holding her hand over her nose.

"It looks to me like it was just one. I think that's what we heard. They generally stay to the shadows and absolutely hate fire. I think he's gone off to forage elsewhere," Annabel added.

Melanie had her fifth or sixth shudder just then. "I can't wait to get out of this place. But you're saying they're now living somewhere in the human world. That means—can they procreate? Could we find more?"

"Not likely. Things from the Underworld don't grow, Melanie. I'm sure you have realized that by now. They don't breed. Someone would have to bring them here."

As they rounded a bend to the right, they both saw what appeared to be the entrance to the tunnel, casting a very faint light several hundred feet ahead of them. The tracks had disappeared, veering off to the left and around a corner. What they saw was a paved road, and at the very end toward the opening, they found a car of some sort, with its doors open. The car appeared abandoned.

"Thank God!" Annabel said.

Melanie too was heartened to be coming to the end of their journey.

Just then, a dark figure blocked their path. Melanie nearly ran into him but stopped just short and grabbed Annabel, pushing her back farther.

Naveen!

"There you are, my pretties. I knew you'd come along."

"Naveen, what are you doing here?"

He chuckled coolly. "I came to pick you up, to give you a hand."

Melanie felt Annabel's hands clutch her cloak. The young guardian was shivering. Still holding the pipe in her right hand, she tightened her grip and got ready to strike if necessary.

"We're not going back, Naveen. Now get out of our way. I'm to deliver this angel on instructions from the director himself."

The slimy bastard grinned, showing off his red-stained teeth. "Nice try, Melanie. I happen to know she's a refugee, an escapee, and I'm paid a big bounty for bringing her back to the fold. Now, if you will step—"

Melanie didn't hesitate. She raised her arm, clutching the pipe in her right hand and slammed it down and across Naveen's head and cheek. He screamed. His blood-curdling, desperate cry for help was not answered. He fell back, trying to kick at the ladies with his long legs and pointed toed shoes as he held his face, which was now spraying blood over both of them. Melanie shielded them both with her cloak, peeking out to make sure he was not going to get up. But he was on his knees, trying to pitch forward and get a foothold. He pressed against the stone walls for balance and was going to succeed.

Melanie knew he was seriously wounded due to his enormous loss of blood, but couldn't take a chance he'd come after them, or get someone else to. Examining the vehicle, she didn't see any movement of an accomplice coming to his aid. So she struck him again in the face, and then hit him repeatedly until he stopped moving.

"Mother of God, Melanie! You've killed him!" Annabel whispered, covering her mouth with her fingers. She appeared to be swooning, dizzy.

Melanie grabbed the lamp and quickly put her arms under the tiny guardian to keep her from falling. "Come on, Annabel. I need you to stay focused. We have to get out of here right away."

Annabel abruptly stopped and wretched, more a reaction than emptying the contents of her stomach. Melanie set the lamp down and held her. The young guardian was sobbing.

"I had to, Annabel. He was going to bring us back."

"But you know what this means, Melanie? It means that whatever Josh's plans are, the director knows about them. He's in grave danger! If they knew about us, then he's down there, all alone, and perhaps about to walk into a trap."

Chapter 15

JOSHUA LEFT HIS meeting with Spencer, returning home, since he'd indicated no meeting had been set up with the Guardian House. He hated to use Spencer in this manner, since he had set up a smooth transition for him into the Underworld, but he knew that was probably done to curry favor with the director. If he had the opportunity, though, he would give Spencer a chance to redeem himself. Father had done that very thing for him. If there was a way he could bestow the same gift and keep everyone he cared for safe, he vowed he would.

He had no idea what Noel was about, though, and that bothered him. On his way back to his rooms, he saw Cass with a group of other people sitting around a large table inside one of the government lobby areas. In the center of the huge room was a statue in some kind of black marble, highly polished.

He watched Cass for a minute before she looked up and noticed him. He didn't have to ask for her attention. She addressed the group, stood, and came outside to greet him.

The sun had gotten much brighter today, so he put on his glasses. His eyes were still sensitive to bright lights. He noted her gait, assured and confident, perhaps thinking he would owe her something for delivering Melanie. He'd have to find out about where she was with everything and knew exactly how to start. She wore a red knit dress and four inch heels—the color of the day, every day now.

"Joshua!" She held her arms out wide, and he allowed her the hug, kissing her on both cheeks. "Don't you look fit, happy, and well serviced!" She winked at that one.

He didn't like the disrespect she implied but removed his glasses anyway.

"How is she? All settled in?"

If Cass knew about the escape, she was adept at covering it up. "She likes it here," he lied. "Keeps asking me all the time if she could open up a flower shop."

Cass frowned and took a step back.

"Flowers? Here?"

Josh shrugged. "It's going to take some getting used to. She still thinks of this place as an enhanced version of home. She'll learn."

Cass didn't flinch, but he watched for any sign of couched behavior.

"I could tell you like them naive." She lowered her voice. "But good for you. I was worried it wouldn't be a good fit. But I think you can have a real future here. And, in time, I think you'd both be quite an asset to the team."

Josh nodded agreement. "I keep meaning to ask you if I could have my key back."

"Oh. Well, I have to check."

It clearly caught her off guard.

He angled his head while he twirled his sunglasses. "Really? *My* key to my *private* residence and you have to check? With whom? And why?" He wasn't going to let her off the hook one bit. He had to know who he could count on.

She had some inner conflict as her usually marbled forehead creased, but then she made a decision. He could see it in her eyes.

"You're completely right. I have it in my briefcase inside. Come in. I'll introduce you to the team, and give it to you." She waved her hand in front of her face. "I don't know what I was thinking."

"No worries," he said as he walked beside her. "You're used to getting permission for lots of things these days. I get it. I completely understand."

"Thank you," she gushed, placing her hand on his left forearm and leaving it there just a tad too long for his comfort.

She opened the glass door for him. "*Entrez!*" she said as she motioned for him to go first.

The large black statue was extremely imposing. It was a perfect likeness of Francisco Kobyashi, except nearly five or six times larger. He sported a smile, and one hand was in the air, giving a very innocuous smile and greeting to everyone who entered. On the far wall were mounted the bronze letters, *Kobyashi Center for Strategic Thinking.* It gave Joshua shivers.

The group at the table was reviewing a set of plans. Most of them wore business attire, suits and long-sleeved shirts, which seemed so out of place. It was more like something he would see in San Francisco or some other large city up top. All of them appeared to be young, handsome, and extremely fresh-faced.

He could remember the years as a dark angel when everyone he met on the street drooled and had bad teeth. Things were indeed changing. He decided not to make a comment of his private thoughts.

"So, this is the legendary Joshua Brandon, who ac-tually is one of our biggest celebrities and knew several of the previous directors. And he also toyed with the idea of—" she pushed up her eyebrows and held her open palm in his direction, seeking him to finish her sentence.

"Never becoming a director," he said, cutting off her line of thinking. "I didn't want the responsibility. And I'd never have been able to mount such an ambitious building campaign." He followed it up with a grin, surprising everyone.

One of the fresh faces stood, extending his hand. "I'm Cory Fieldstone. My father is a big builder in Texas. I'm glad you've decided to join us. It's all quite extraordinary, isn't it?"

Joshua wondered why the son of a successful builder would choose to live in the Underworld, since he didn't appear to be the free spirit most the new recruits had been in his day.

"Well, I'm just flattered to be welcomed. I'm not sure what I can do, but I'm looking forward to finding a productive place on one of your teams."

As Cass pulled out the small brown envelope that contained his key, she said to the others, "Now you see why I was so excited we were helping to bring his girlfriend. And Joshua says she wishes to open up a flower shop."

She handed him the envelope as all heads looked up to her in rapt attention, but no one smiled. In fact, they all looked like they'd been sucker punched.

After a few anxious moments, young Fieldstone continued, "Well, enjoy the rest of your day and we'll see you soon, I'm sure. The Underworld is not complete without the addition of the legendary Joshua Brandon. We've all heard the stories, sir. I am honored." He bowed, and then took his seat at the table. The discussion continued without any further delay. Cass took her place and gave him a wink and a winning smile.

Josh needed a drink. Thankfully, Cass had left some waters and a couple other little bottles in their refrigerator they hadn't touched. He hoped there was something in there with some kind of elixir or alcohol.

As he made his way back to the room, he pondered why he was suddenly so upset. Life for most the people he ran across had improved greatly. He wasn't sure what went on in the back alleyways at night, especially in neighborhoods where the Pink Pineapple was located, but the makeover being conducted here gave the illusion of a modern city up top. He knew the type of inhabitants well from his centuries growing up, and he got the impression the population, now recruited below, was to become minions. He knew that some of the reason some people wound up here was because that was the opposite of what they wanted out of life.

Kobyashi's imprint was on everything.

He tested Cass' key to make sure he hadn't received the wrong one, and found it worked perfectly. He nearly ran to the refrigerator and opened it up, finding a small pint of RedX and some potato chips. He wasn't hungry, but he wanted to gnash his teeth on something. And he wanted to get a little tipsy, too.

He knew Melanie wouldn't be there, but after he'd dulled his brain a bit, he sadly searched the empty room from the comfort of his now-empty bed. The place where he'd be sleeping alone. The place that smelled of her.

He retrieved another drink because the first one had made him morose. It also enhanced her scent, and it made him miss her more, anxious to know that nothing ill had befallen her. He set the bottle down on the bedside table and ran to the back door, moving aside the drapes and turned the latch, opening him to the tunnel. Light from his fireplace showered across the sidewalk, over the old tracks, and beyond. But the more he looked, the blacker and denser it got.

"Mel?" he whispered. "Are you here?"

Nothing answered him except the low growling moan from the wind.

The second bottle did little to help settle him, so he decided to leave early for the Guardian House and perhaps stop along the way somewhere for something stronger than he had in his room. He was sitting in a tiny space with no windows, cut off from everyone in his life he cared about, not knowing if they got out, feeling outnumbered and outplayed. Was this all an exercise in futility? He began to wonder if his mission wasn't doomed to failure.

He threw the extra key in a drawer, double-checked the back-door lock after peeking into the tunnel one more time, with the same results as before. He adjusted the fire down low and took one more look at the place that had held such happiness for him. He'd spend the brightest day and night of his life here. Maybe she was right. Maybe they should have done this together. Then at least, they could have a few more stolen hours or minutes.

Closing the door behind him, he leaned back, breathing in the dark air that began to feel toxic, claustrophobic. Searching to his right and left, the street was vacant. But he heard people gathering somewhere. And that's where he headed.

A group of tables sat in the afternoon sun. Couples dressed up were sipping cool drinks. He felt like he'd fallen into a Hallmark movie. The tables were clean, and the people wore nicely pressed clothes. The filth of the streets had been replaced with wide esplanades and brand new lighted storefronts, selling electronics, clothing—anything that wasn't alive. No pet stores, no florists, and very little in the way of foods. There were snacks laced with CBD, elixirs, and aphrodisiacs, oils, salves, and other necessary stimulants for peak performance.

What did the people who couldn't afford all this do? Had they been removed to some human dump somewhere? Where had the men and women who roamed the streets and slept in park benches gone?

One after another, he saw people gathered in groups, laughing. Couples dressed in costumes, lovers of every sexual orientation. They were eye candy, because he didn't feel like he belonged here. It was a familiar feeling. He hadn't felt he belonged in the human world either.

Jazz music from one of his favorite hangouts blared into the daytime reverie. A couple was dancing. Others clapped to the rhythm. The dive had been called Pete's and it still was. The old sign was still there, but that's the only thing that remained of the jazz house he'd spent many nights in. And Pete's never was open in the middle of the day either.

He saw the big sign advertising RedX in neon at the next watering hole, and he slipped inside, sat up to the bar, and ordered a double with whiskey chaser. On second thought, he drank the whiskey first, then the RedX, and asked for another whiskey. He turned to survey the room and didn't recognize anyone. He searched the shadows, usually able to find someone from his past, but the lighting didn't create any shadows, no places to hide out.

The RedX was starting to make his ears buzz. His visual acuity improved. He heard conversations outside the little dive. Across the plaza, water splashed. Someone was crying in the distance, and he heard a couple kissing.

One of the night ladies sauntered up to him and asked if he was lonely.

"I am as a matter of fact. But no, I'm not interested in company. I'm not very good company right now."

"I can change your mind." She started to reach for him, but he grabbed her forearm.

"I said no."

"You don't have to feel bad about it. Everyone has a low day. That's what I do." She was trying to be attractive, alluring. She wasn't very good at it.

"I'm not the kind of date you want."

"Just one kiss, friend. Friend to friend?"

He smiled. He knew the difference between the man he was today and the man he'd been before. It actually gave him a sense of pride to understand that, and to say, "No thank you. I'm sure there's someone else out there more deserving than I."

He left money on the counter for a drink for her and left.

Several places down was a coffee house and he ordered an espresso. The bitter taste actually dissolved the remains of the RedX as he felt the effects finally wane. He ordered one more, and then left with the paper cup between his fingers, headed toward the river bridge and the big house.

As he crossed the plaza, he wondered if he was being followed, so he turned right and meandered through another row of shops, looking in the windows for any reflection of someone following him. He didn't pick up anyone. Back and forth he went, even reversing course and walking back down one street he'd been on from the opposite side. No one looked to be interested in him at all. He took a path to the river's edge and followed it until the bridge was in sight.

He could see a guardian sitting on a park bench in the small garden outside the front doors. He bobbed a bit to the right and left, hoping to catch her eye, but she didn't see him. She stood and rubbed her elbows and upper arms, warming herself as she paced back and forth.

Not seeing anyone else, Josh stepped over the

guardrail at the river's edge, walked down the embankment, and followed the river until he came to the bridge abutments. He spotted a set of steps, scaled them, and was not more than ten feet from the angel.

She jumped.

"Didn't mean to scare you."

"You're Joshua Brandon?"

"I am."

"Quick. They're waiting for us inside. I'm Molly, by the way." Before opening the doors, she checked over her shoulder and then let him go inside ahead of her.

He found a group of a half dozen guardians and two men. Several of the group rose and came forward, shaking his hand and introducing themselves. One by one, he remembered some of them. Their faces had become lost in his past, but now, as they stood before him, he remembered. It was sobering to look into the faces of former guardians, women whose lives he forever altered.

"Thank you for agreeing to meet with us. We weren't sure you would." She extended her hand and Joshua took it. "I'm Gerry. Sort of the unofficial spokesman of this group. I realize this is a very strange situation for you."

"To say the least," he answered. "I admit I almost didn't come."

"I'll be blunt," Gerry continued, "We think we've been targeted for extermination. Not just some of us, but all of us."

He saw that no one looked away. Their gaze was riveted on him.

"And, Mr. Brandon, we don't have much time. We've all decided to take a stand. Whatever is our fate, we're going to do it in one large group."

"Take a stand?"

"We're going to start an armed insurrection if we have to."

"But you'll get wiped out. There's no way anyone will survive."

"Then so be it. That will be our last act of goodwill, then," answered one of the men.

"But that's suicide!"

Most of the crowd smiled, and then it hit him. They'd all willingly given up their human lives to gain admittance to the Underworld in the first place. They'd done it before.

"This time, Joshua, we stand for something. Someone has to do what we were charged with doing when we were originally created. Someone has to protect the human population," said Gerry.

Several of the others nodded in agreement.

Joshua's mind was racing. He didn't comprehend

fully what she was trying to tell him. He shook his head. "This is hard to take in. What makes you think you're being targeted? And what does this have to do with things up top. What proof do you have?"

One of the two men spoke up next. "You've seen the buildings, the banners. Mr. Kobyashi has put together a cabal, a committee of people who are going to help him gain full control of the Underworld. They are harnessing power and bringing the population together. Those that don't go along, just disappear."

"I see it. I myself am surprised how fast it's changed. I can barely recognize some of the older districts. It's cleaner, well lit. The Underworld was a very dangerous place at one time. Creatures flew through the sky breathing fire. The Director himself was vaporizing those who disagreed with him. I was involved in his takedown."

"It's even more dangerous now," said Gerry. "It just doesn't look that way. It's under the surface, hidden. But we've seen some of it. We know more than they think we know."

"They're raising more of those creatures as we speak," said one of the women. "You just don't see them out and about. Not yet. But they're raising an army of genetically modified beings. Disposable creatures."

"But there would be the signs—" Josh started to protest.

"You've seen the statues, the banners. The testimonials. The way they talk about the directorate like its some great government program of prosperity. The requirement for meetings, for example," said another person.

"It's hard for me to fathom," he finally said. "Where is your proof?"

"We know this, Josh. We've seen the plans. After they finish their building and organization here, they intend to take over the human world next. By that time, they will be so powerful with their special abilities, brought about through genetic mutation and their sheer numbers of supporters on both sides. We have families now sending part of their family here to learn, to liaison with those up top. They do it so they can be at the front of the line when the spoils are delivered."

"You actually think there's coordination between the worlds?"

"Yes," the group said in unison.

He wondered why he had not heard any of this before. He also wondered why Father had neglected to tell him.

"Francisco Kobyashi's a brilliant thinker. Maybe it's a crazy idea, but he's closing all the holes in his net, and now he's tightening the noose. Maybe he'll fail. But he rules by intimidation and fear. And he'll eliminate everyone who will get in his way. That's why we're a target. After they take us, who will stand up to them? Who, Joshua?" Gerry asked.

He realized they could be right. But the scale of the project became impossible to comprehend. There was no way he could help with this. He was totally out of his league.

"What is it you want from me? I'm incapable of mounting any campaign like you talk about. I have no experience with it. I've no talent. And I'm not a fucking hero." He lowered his head and apologized.

The group got deathly silent. The at last someone had the nerve to speak up.

"We know this isn't your fight. It's ours. We just want you to *try* to get us out," said the leader. "Since you are the reason most of us came here in the first place, we thought you might see your way to reversing that action somewhat. Just try, Joshua. That's all we ask." Gerry's eyes were steady and didn't reveal an ounce of beg. She was all heart, forward action. No regret, no wavering in her decision to live free or die trying.

Josh surveyed the group. "Why don't you just go? Couldn't you bribe your way past the monitors? People used to do this all the time when permissions were revoked. There was always a back doorway to do this."

"They won't let us leave. Many have tried. Several have never returned," she said.

"Maybe they got out."

"No, we've confirmed it. Guardians are going missing every day. It's time for us to fight. We need to fight our way out," said one of the men.

Josh counted eight or nine guardians. He knew Father intended he bring them all home. So, there must be an additional twenty or more elsewhere. But this group, if he had a little help, might be possible to smuggle out. But then that would dash his chances to get the others out.

"There must be more of you somewhere," he said, overlooking the little group.

"Some have disappeared, as I've said," Gerry began. "A handful do not want to go, and that's a problem because we aren't sure we can trust them. But yes, there are more. More guardians and others who want to go as well. Come this way, please."

Josh followed along with the group surrounding him. They walked down a set of stairs. At the bottom, Gerry pushed open two double doors and stepped into a large auditorium. It was filled with a sea of cots and bedrolls. He estimated there were over two hundred individuals in the room.

"We need to get everybody out."

Chapter 16

MELANIE AND ANNABEL arrived at Jonas and Audray's home near dark. Melanie's cloak hid some of Naveen's blood, and she'd used it to wipe off her face and arms. Her chest was spattered in it. Jonas answered the door and quickly pulled them both inside.

"Holy shit, ladies. What the hell—?"

"Thank you so much. Josh sent us. I didn't have anywhere else to go."

"No, you did the right thing," mumbled Jonas. He checked the street for signs they were followed and then closed the door behind them.

Audray ran up to Melanie and gave her a big hug. "Oh, Melanie. I was so happy to learn you and Josh were—" She noticed the state of her bloody clothes. "Oh my God, what's happened?"

"We had some trouble. Listen, we have nowhere else to stay. This is Annabel, one of Josh's guardians. She helped me get out."

"Welcome, Annabel. Of course you can stay," she said.

"Whose blood is this?" Jonas asked.

"Naveen Broadchurch. He was the one who brought me to Joshua in the first place. He tried to block our return here. He was going to drag us back, both of us."

"Where is he now, and is he alive?"

Melanie lowered her eyes, shaking her head. "I left him in the tunnel."

"She's convinced Naveen was sent by the director himself," added Annabel.

Jonas examined Melanie's arms, her hands. "Are you hurt anywhere?"

"No. I struck him with a piece of pipe. We exited the back way,"

"Ah, so you were in Josh's quarters, then. The infamous little room." Jonas' face lit up in recognition. "I've been there."

"It's how Naveen brought me in. And Josh asked us to leave that way so we wouldn't have to go through a transport station and be reported," offered Annabel.

"Come on, ladies, and let's have you shower and then get some clean clothes on you." Audray lifted the cloak off Melanie. "Jonas, get the kids ready for supper while I get them washed up, okay? I don't want them to see this."

"Sure thing. I'll be right back." They heard Jonas' footsteps run down the wooden hallway, making the whole house shake.

"I've got extra towels up there, and I'll dig out some sweats for you both. It's the first bedroom to the right at the top of the stairs. I'll bring some things in just a minute."

The shower felt heavenly. Audray had a pair of sweats lying on the bed for each of them. Annabel was so tiny she had to cinch the pants in order to keep them from sliding off.

"Wish there was some way we could get word to Josh we arrived." Melanie was towel drying her hair. She knew their telepathy would not stretch beyond one world or the other.

Annabel nodded. "Maybe Jonas knows someone who goes back and forth. Someone must."

"Well, that was Spencer and Noel, but now I don't know."

Annabel sat on the bed. "Do you suppose Josh has met with the House angels?"

"He said he was going to. I know he will try to at least," Melanie answered. She was thinking about the words Annabel had said about the director knowing Josh was on a mission.

"Do you think Naveen could have been sent by someone else?" she asked. "He said he was being paid a bounty. Maybe it was a private arrangement. There are so many factions, it seems. Maybe someone else was up to that, or maybe he took it on himself. Could he have been the one following you?"

"It's possible. But I think you should assume the worst. We need to somehow get Josh some help."

Melanie agreed. "We'll see what Jonas says. Are you okay staying here if they ask us?"

"I have no one anymore. The human world is completely foreign to me, Melanie. I'm hoping this will be a good place to stay until the others come. And then I'll sort it out."

They tiptoed downstairs and greeted Jonas and Audray's beautiful children. Melanie couldn't tear her eyes off them.

"Are you friends from Dad's old job too?" one of the twins asked.

"I am. We both are," Melanie answered.

Jonas inserted himself. "Melanie here is Josh's lady friend. And this is her friend—from work."

Audray asked if they needed anything, and both the girls declined but accepted ice water.

"Jonas, why don't you take them to the living room? I'm going to help the kids finish and clean up the kitchen. You guys, I'll join you when I'm finished."

"I should help you. You've been so kind," said Annabel.

"Nonsense. We're all in this together. Josh would do the same for us in a heartbeat. Now go, please."

They sat on the couch across from the large leather recliner that obviously was Jonas'. He started the fireplace. The heat felt marvelous.

"Thank you so much, first of all," Melanie began. "I wasn't sure, and now that I see the kids. You're taking a risk—"

"Hogwash. Audray's already told you if it were reversed, Josh would have done the same, and you know it. So, what the heck is going on down there?" Jonas asked. "Noel said all hell's breaking loose."

"You saw him?" Melanie asked.

"He came by about an hour before you arrived." Jonas squinted. "Tell me. Tell me all of it."

Annabel rushed in first. "You can't trust him, Jonas. He works for the director. He's dangerous."

"Noel? No way." Jonas' voice boomed, nearly rattling the windows.

"Truth is, Jonas, we don't know who to trust," added Melanie. "There's so much confusion. It's pure chaos."

"Well, that's nothing new, at least," Jonas answered.

"But they have this new director who is putting everything on lockdown. We think all Joshua's former guardians are in danger." She rubbed the tears from her cheeks. "He's all alone down there. It's just him against a very powerful group. I'm so worried about him, Jonas."

He studied her. "Why don't you trust Spencer and Noel? He delivered Joshua safely on my orders. You two were reunited. They did that as a favor to me. I've trusted them with the lives of my children."

"No, Jonas. We think it was all a plan." Melanie knew it wasn't what he wanted to hear.

"But I called them. They've protected this house on many occasions. I just don't buy it."

"All the guardians are scared, Mr. Jonas, that they're going to be sacrificed," said Annabel. "Director Kobyashi has big plans everyone's been whispering about. He's building huge projects, schools, a factory, a sports arena. Josh couldn't believe how much it had changed. They're supposed to announce the master plan this week. They've created zones for industries there, jobs for people. It's all being organized by this committee. And everyone is required to participate. Those who are outsiders are cast out or disappear. There's a lot of fear, and people aren't given the same freedom to go back and forth like Spencer and Noel do."

Annabel sat back and let it sink in.

"What she's saying is true. Maybe they've only recently been recruited to go to the dark side, Jonas, but Josh feels their loyalties are compromised. He wanted me to be sure to tell you that," Melanie added.

"What did Noel want?" Annabel asked.

"He told me he wondered if I'd heard from Josh. Told me the two of you got connected, that Josh was happy. But he did say there was a lot of shit going on, things shifting in the wind, that sort of thing. But hell, I've lived down there, I know what it's like. It's always like that. He didn't say anything about you escaping. He gave no indication of that at all. I guess he has a little friend here he visits." Then Jonas shrugged, "Ladies, it all sounded innocent to me."

"Still, you should be careful. Don't tell him about us," begged Melanie.

"What about Spencer?" Jonas asked.

"I think Josh is more worried about Spencer, to be honest," Melanie began. "He's been a regular at the directorship meetings. And he told Josh that the director had special plans for him, whatever that means."

Jonas got up and paced the living room floor.

"They have said the Underworld has cleaned up a lot. Are you sure this all isn't a good thing?"

"If it's all a good thing, then why did Josh send me back here, Jonas?" Melanie asked.

"Good point. And if what you say is true, Josh is in it all by himself." He stared into the fire. "I'm tempted to lend him a hand," he whispered. "He's going to need an ally."

"No, sir. You are not going down there, Jonas," Audray said from the doorway. "That's not an option. If it was dangerous for Melanie, it's too dangerous for you."

"Audray's right, Jonas. Josh and I even discussed that your two colleagues are perfectly positioned to enlist your help, so they can use you too. He feels like I was used as bait to lure him back there. With Josh in trouble, perhaps, there's a lure to get you back."

"But why me? What point would that make?"

"Because you're married to a former director," Audray answered. "They want us both."

Annabel cleared her throat. "If I may speak plainly, my boss, Helena, thinks once he masters all of the Underworld, Mr. Kobyashi has his designs on the human world. He's building an army of fire breathers—"

"Oh God," Audray sat, putting her face in her hands.

"Melanie found one, or at least we heard one of them in the tunnel. That's on the human side. My friends at the Guardian House have seen the prototypes they're building. They're readying for war."

Jonas turned to Melanie. "And your Joshua thinks he can stop all this? He's got to be crazy!"

"No crazier than you thinking you can join him," added Audray. "Jonas, I forbid you. This isn't your war. And if it is coming, then you'll be needed here. Even the two of you or ten of you couldn't stop them, if that's what they want to do. They have enormous powers in that realm."

"But we can't just let him die," Jonas whispered back.

"He has lots of allies in the guardians, Jonas. They're ready to fight. Maybe that will be enough," said Annabel.

Jonas shook his head.

Melanie was hanging on every word, her stomach doing flip-flops. She saw a vision, a picture of wholesale death and destruction. Burning worlds and elimination of civilizations, the apocalypse in real time, coming to claim everything and everyone. She'd made a decision and surprised herself at her resolve. Quietly at first, she spoke her peace.

"If anyone goes back, it's me. Tell me what to do, Jonas. What do I need to bring him?"

Chapter 17

J OSH'S HEAD WAS irritating him until he realized he'd been in a near-coma in bed and someone was banging on his door. He slipped on a pair of boxers and padded to the door, opening it just a crack.

Spencer stood there, his hands on his hips. He pressed the door open with force, swearing.

"Well, good morning to you too. Maybe you didn't have the kind of night I had, but I didn't even fuckin' ask you in. What's so goddamned urgent?" Josh spat.

Spencer eyed the bed. "Where's Melanie?"

"That's a very good question. She didn't come home last night. That's why I'm feeling a little under the weather today, so if you don't mind—What the hell are you doing here this early?"

"Shopping," he said pointing to his watch. "Remember the party tonight at the director's? I'm in charge of getting you looking your best, and I do have other things to do, so hurry up. Get dressed and let's go. And we can look for her while we're at it."

Either Spencer didn't know where she was or he was very good at lying. He doubted the latter. So, he decided to play along as if they'd had a fight.

"Jeez. I just broke up with my lady and you are worrying about what to wear at a party tonight.

"No, not me, remember. You're going to the party. I'm probably taking out the trash or some dumb shit."

Josh slipped on his pants. "What's gotten into you, Spencer? Did I do something wrong other than try to sleep in on your watch? You my guard dog or something? Melanie would have kicked your butt for that."

"What did you do?"

Josh decided it was time to embellish the story. He remembered the wandering women last night. If he had been watched, someone would have seen him drinking and meandering around the place. He rolled his shoulder. "You forget I've had a pretty good time here. Maybe you wouldn't understand, but I think she was jealous. She just wants to show me she's independent, you know. Like she doesn't need me as much as I need her?"

"And that's why I'm staying single."

Josh doubted that. "No, it's because you're mean."

"Come on, man. Let's go."

"God, you'd think it was a national emergency."

As he finished getting dressed, he thought about

the enormous burden he carried, the promises he'd made to a whole warehouse full of people he didn't know how to fulfill. The idea of going shopping in the middle of all that made him sick. And he still hadn't heard anything about Melanie and whether they'd safely passed to the human world.

Spencer was fingering things in his refrigerator without asking.

"Hey. You moving in now?"

"Just checking."

"I drank the RedX last night. We'll pick some up today."

"Suit yourself. Ready?"

"Yup." He grabbed his key, slipping it into his pants pocket, and they were outside walking the streets in seconds.

"So, where did you leave her?" Spencer asked as they passed by several stores that had not yet opened.

"Actually, we were to meet by the fountain, and she never showed. I came back, found she wasn't here, and went out looking for her. I had a little too much fun, I guess. I expected her to be here when I got back but no."

Spencer stopped in his tracks. "You don't suppose she's escaped."

Josh wrinkled his nose. "Nah. We had a little argument, that's all. I even think she might have gone over to Helena's. I'll check there after we're done. It will all be fine, you'll see."

"The director is expecting you both, you know."

"I know. She's actually looking forward to it." The lies were getting easier now. He fell into a healthy banter with Spencer, who he could have been friends with under other circumstances. Josh began to relax, which he needed for clear thinking. They'd set into motion a plan last night he honestly didn't think would work. But if the element of surprise remained on their side, perhaps they could pull it off.

As they entered a busier part of the city, Josh tucked away his thoughts for fear there would be a mind reader in their midst.

"Where are we going?" he asked.

"You've got an appointment with the director's tailor." Spencer pulled out a silver card that glistened in the sunlight. "And the director said to fix you right up."

"He's paying for this?"

"Yes, sir. For Melanie's dress too, if you want to stop and get something for her."

"Wow. He takes his fashion seriously," Josh said, fishing for answers.

"He takes everything seriously. You're the man of

the hour, Joshua Brandon. He's got you on display, which is a good thing for you. Make the most of it, and if you're lucky and sufficiently grateful, your future could be written in diamonds," he said, pulling out the card again.

They entered a gentleman's store and were greeted by a clerk with thick glasses and a tape measure hanging around his neck.

"I am Donaldo, special tailor to the director. You are Mr. Brandon, I assume?"

"Yes, sir, he is," Spencer rudely interrupted. "You're to find something very elegant, very flashy for our celebrity guest tonight."

"Oh, tonight? My goodness, we'll have to find something already made. I have no time for a fully—"

"We know," Spencer interrupted.

"Look, just show me what you have on the rack. I'm easy to please. Trust me."

The little clerk took them to the back, and after measuring the length of Josh's arms and his back and chest, directed them to a rack of sport jackets suitable for a rock star. He held a navy-blue jacket with baby blue rhinestones filling in the entire label on both sides.

"Ew!" Josh said and pushed the jacket away. "Not my style at all."

"But you must pick one from this collection. If it is

ready-wear and you are a special guest of the director, then these are the clothes you will wear."

It wasn't an invitation to pick. It was a command, he noted.

"Where are the ones without all the crusty stuff?" he asked.

"These are what you are to wear, Mr. Brandon. And since I believe you are not paying for it, you should feel grateful. Mr. Kobyashi wouldn't like it if you defied him."

Josh noted the little man was nervous. The consequences of his choice would weigh heavily on this man as well.

He flipped through the coats and selected a white dinner jacket with a minimal number of sequins and rhinestones. No bright colors, just the bling. He chose a black pair of slacks and a pair of beautiful hand-made pumps made from crocodile.

The clerk added a white silk handkerchief for his lapel pocket, carefully placed everything in a zipped hangar bag, and handed it to him. Spencer presented the card, and the little man tapped a screen and handed it back to him.

"I thank you very much. I hope you'll come back and take a look at some other things very soon, Mr. Brandon. And when you are not in such a hurry, I will make you the finest suit you've ever worn. It will fit you like a second skin and make you feel like a king!"

Joshua knew he was right. It was the first thing he liked about the changes to the Underworld.

They selected a red satin dress for Melanie in her size with shoes to match. He wasn't sure about the shoe size, but he knew the dress would fit fabulously if only she were really going to appear.

Spencer seemed to be satisfied he'd done his job. Before parting, he handed Josh a card with the director's home address on it, along with the director's personal phone number.

"I believe you said you got a phone?"

"I did."

"He'd like you to call when you are on your way, please."

Josh stared at Spencer. "Why?"

"Those are just his instructions. I'm doing as I've been told."

"So what are you doing tonight?" Josh asked.

"I'm hoping to find Noel, but something will come up. It always does."

"Just so we're clear, you now work for the director, is that right?"

He nodded.

"What about Jonas?"

"I never worked for Jonas. I followed him. We rode bikes together. We did stuff. I was just part of his crew."

"Doing what exactly?"

Spencer gave a wide, red grin. "Whatever the hell we wanted. Those were some fun days, all pre-Audray, of course. You were here then, in the beginning, you remember?"

"I do. So tell me, are you having as much fun now?"

"This isn't about fun."

"I gathered that. But, have you ever stopped to think what your life would be like if you could return to those days?"

"And give up all this progress? No, this is a calling. We're making a world here. We're making it better for everyone, and you can see it. People are dressed nice. They have money to spend. Not like what it used to be like. Addictions are down. Less people dying—their second death—on the streets. It's a good thing."

Josh thought about that conversation all the way to Helena's.

It isn't about fun, Spencer had said. Josh wondered what the point of it all was, then.

HELENA WAS HAPPY to see him and greeted him like she used to, at the top of her grand staircase. The gardens in front were lush and beautiful, as always. The girls were pretty, walking past him, catching his eyes, expecting to be chosen. But Josh wanted to talk to Helena and told them so. She called him upstairs to her rooms.

She was wearing red again. Everything in her boudoir was red, except for a brief phase when she liked hot pink for some reason. She poured him a glass of RedX and a glass of water for herself.

"Is it safe to talk here?" he whispered.

"I've got scramblers, if that's what you're wondering. And I don't tape sessions, so yes, we're free to talk."

"I think they got out yesterday. I've received no word yet, but if it had been a disaster, well, I would have certainly heard about it."

"Thank you."

"So, I'd like to ask you to be my date tonight. I'm going to dinner at the Director's house." He pointed to the bags of clothes on the floor by the door.

"Why do you need me there?"

"There may come a time when you can leave with some people who are going to, that's all. Bring your jewels, your money, and anything else you don't want to part with."

"You're serious? You wouldn't joke with me about

this, would you?"

Josh was happy to tell her he wouldn't. "But I can't tell you it's foolproof. The less you know, the better it will be for you. My ruse is that Melanie has gone missing, ran off with someone else temporarily because we had a fight. You're my replacement date to make her jealous."

"Would that were the case, Josh," she said and smiled. It warmed Josh's heart. He wanted to see her free from all this.

"That ship sailed a long time ago, Helena. We had the best we could have. Those days we had freedom to choose. Now, we have just freedom. That's what I'm hoping to be able to offer you tonight. You should take it and never look back."

She teared up, but like a lady, she used a tissue to keep from messing her makeup. Her garnet earrings glinted in the sunlight, as always. Joshua wondered if she ever took them off.

"Will there be a sign, then? How?"

"Oh, you'll know. Trust me, you'll know."

He got up to leave, and she embraced him. "I may not ever get this chance in private again, but Joshua Brandon, thank you for being the love of my life for nearly a hundred years. Can you believe it's been that long?"

He planted a tender kiss on her red lips, which began a series of familiar things happening to his body, not unpleasant. But he smiled and stepped back, releasing her. From his safe distance, he told her, "And you, lovely Helena, have been like fine wine. You get better and better with the passage of time. Your vintage is rare indeed. We've never argued, have we?"

"No, never."

"We've never talked about the future, have we?"

"No." She dropped her smile.

"But we've enjoyed each other, and I have to say I also have loved you. If this works, your freedom couldn't even slightly repay you for all the years of affection you've shown me. I sometimes wonder if I ever would have made it here without you."

He gave her the card from the director and told her to show up at seven where he'd be waiting. He left her standing there, as perfect as she'd ever be. She wasn't Melanie, but she was someone who deserved more than she was dealt.

Chapter 18

J OSH'S NEXT STOP was the clockmaker. Manfred's sign said open, but the door was locked. Upon hearing him jiggling the handle, his swarm slipped between the crack under the front door and the frame, buzzing menacingly over his head, just out of danger of being swatted.

Manfred's apron was covered in blood. His hands wore bright blue rubber gloves, also bloody.

"I'm in surgery. Come back later," the inventor shouted through the front door.

"I can't." Josh leaned down at the clockmaker's level to make sure they were making eye contact. The little man's eyelids blinked, enhanced by the large magnification. His eyes moved from side to side as he studied Josh's face and then made his decision.

He held up one bloody finger and disappeared.

Seconds later, a semi-lifelike looking robot showed up at the door, a female model with enhanced body parts, full red lips, and bright red hair. At her right shoulder, an arm was missing, and blood streamed down the side of her naked body. Josh realized she'd been the one in surgery. The sight of wires and bluish white tendrils extending from her arm socket turned Josh's stomach. But mostly he was in shock.

She turned the lock, stepped back without looking at him, and let Josh inside.

"I didn't realize—"

"Oh, shut up and get inside quickly. I'll talk to you while I finish. Mandy! Close and lock the door."

The female did as she was told. She followed behind as Manfred made his way back to the surgery room.

"You gave me a start there, boss. For a minute I thought you'd told me to shut up." Her voice was sexy, raspy, and full of desire. Josh immediately whipped his head around to make sure she hadn't been replaced with a real woman or angel.

She smiled at his reaction. "What, you think a sex toy can't have private thoughts? Shouldn't speak her mind?"

Her program was giving her lots of attitude. Josh kind of liked it.

"Manfred, you've been holding out on me. You've gotten advanced."

"Tell me about it. Desperate is more like it."

The little inventor turned the corner, his brown slippers sliding on the wooden floor. The swarm still hovered over Josh's head.

"She's *yours*?" Josh asked, turning to look at her again. Her flawless skin had an inner glow, all her parts were slightly enhanced; her lips were fuller and more succulent, her nipples were pert and knotted to perfection, her mound—well, he didn't want to look at her that way, but found he couldn't stop. Her nether lips were hairless, flush and slightly pink, engorged for maximum satisfaction, he noted.

She raised her left eyebrow, unafraid to look him in the eyes, as she was no-doubt programmed.

"Tell him, Mandy."

"Sure thing, boss. I love this little cupcake. He makes crazy love to me, and nothing pleases me more than holding his perfect little body against mine as he spills. He is the man I've always wanted, warts and all."

Manfred started to laugh. "I liked that line."

Mandy angled her head in defiance of Josh's shocked face. "Am I enough woman for you to believe?"

"You are more woman than half the mortal women I've had up top."

"We're—"

"Mandy, stop!" Manfred yelled at her.

"Oops," she said, again raising that left brow and placing her only hand over her mouth.

"Mandy, open the door," Manfred commanded.

"Pardon me," she said to Josh, slipping past him, slightly touching his thigh with hers. And then she was in front of them, her perfectly formed butt checks shaking in all the right ways as she moved.

She bent down, used her one hand to open the surgical door, and stepped inside. "Shall I assume the position, boss?"

"Yes, we must finish at once."

Josh hung his jacket bag and the shopping bag on one of the chains suspended from an overhead rack and stared at the scene. Her new arm was prepped, laying on an extension of the surgical table, ready to be attached. Mandy announced she was going to sleep and closed her eyes.

"Sorry about all the blood, Josh. But I gotta finish her in a couple of minutes or I have to re-infuse all her fluids. I have a special cocktail I use with a member I'm attaching so it will want to join quickly with the rest of her body. And it can putrefy if not used within an hour."

"No problem. If this wasn't important, I wouldn't have come."

"You said that. Now get to the point." He started a

high-speed drill, and anything Josh would say would be drowned out.

Josh waited. When the drill stopped, Manfred looked up at him.

"You were saying?"

"Is it safe to talk in here."

"Yes, scrambled and double scrambled. Go ahead."

"There's an armed insurrection coming."

"Oh fuck, they've been talking about that for years now. Those little guardian troublemakers? Don't trust a word they say. I could draw more blood with my swarm," he said, nodding to the group, who took a lap around his head in praise for his words.

"They're emotional. You've given them emotions."

"Sort of," Manfred said as he moved a large magnification arm over the area he was working on. "More like that of a dog. Happy to see me. Require very little maintenance except acknowledgement every once in a while. Territorial and protective."

"So, I've noticed."

"So, you think they're really going to do it this time? You know they've tried before and failed?"

"When?"

"Last year, only a handful of them. It was painful. The director's first public execution. By fire too. Kind of put the pall on the whole movement, if you ask me.

Not that they don't still feel cheated out of their positions here. But he doesn't trust them."

"I don't think he trusts anybody. But this time, Manfred, they've got numbers."

"Interesting. So why tell me this?"

"I want your help. I'm going to get their freedom."

Manfred stopped, his hands holding metal instruments in mid-air. He began to laugh.

"You think it's funny?"

"Not at all. I was right about you. I tell Mandy this all the time."

"And?"

"I tell her you're the Underworld's Messiah."

Chapter 19

JOSH USED THE transport tram to the party. He'd memorized the director's phone number and called him exactly thirty minutes before he was to arrive. The man didn't pick up, which solved another problem. Josh didn't want to lie about Melanie on the phone for fear he'd hear it in his voice. He was duly respectful of what the director possessed.

The tram was filled with other partygoers, mostly young girls, dressed in formal attire. Some couples, occasionally in costume, were seated throughout the three cars that soared to the entrance. As soon as he stepped out, he felt like he was in Disneyland. A large fireworks display was going on. The red modern structure was massive with a wide series of steps adorned with colorful flags with symbols on them. It was as if he was stepping into a soccer field stadium, walking past the flags of competing teams.

He liked the feel of his new clothes, and the rhinestones on his jacket caught many an eye. After he climbed the top step, he saw Helena waiting for him. Again, she was dressed in a deep red, nearly the exact color of the director's castle. She wore a dazzling display of jewels around her neck.

"Stunning, but I expected no less. Look at all the bling!" He kissed her smiling cheeks on both sides.

"You said bring it on, so I did. And look at you. In white. Joshua, that's breathtaking. I'd always thought your color was black."

"Not really my personality and sort of chosen for me, but I'm learning to like it." He searched the bevy of couples and groups climbing the stairs and entering the large foyer beyond where he could see waiters ushering trays of red liquor around to everyone. He recognized several as being guardians he'd spoken to before, but eye contact was minimal and he remained careful.

"Tell me," he said as he grabbed her arm. "Do you have any idea what the occasion is? I was led to believe this was dinner at the director's house. But this, this is an event."

"I think you have something to do with that, Josh."

He shuddered, his mind getting stuck on one picture of how this could all go so wrong. "I hope not."

"Somehow, I don't think you'll disappoint," she whispered to his ear. "Is everything ready?"

"I'm only in charge of the distraction, and the showing up part. I hope all the pieces are working together. Once the curtain goes up, we'll find out."

At the open doorway, he announced himself and Helena and took two drinks, one for each of them. He stepped onto a highly polished black marble floor. A grand staircase curved off to the second floor wing to their right. To the left was where all the partygoers were located. Josh tossed down his RedX and placed it on a tray, attempting to collect another but was rebuffed by a gloved hand. Immediately, a young guardian came with a silver tray and presented him his drink. Then he continued with Helena on his arm, into a large ballroom bordered with floor to ceiling glass windows that had accordioned back to each side, opening the whole room to an outside patio overlooking lit grounds. The large pond below held an enormous fountain in the middle of it.

The two of them stood in the night air, sipping their champaign while watching fireworks going off in the distance.

Nothing on this grand scale had ever been built before, Josh realized. He was witnessing history in the making. It spoke to power and control. The people milling about were the bling, the trim on the decoration clearly meant to impress anyone with a brain.

"I had no idea he lived like this," whispered Helena. She sipped her drink and deposited it on a silver tray presented to her, declining another. "I'm nervous. This place makes me nervous."

"Well, the die is cast. At least we'll be together," Josh whispered, trying to reflect a casual air. But he felt the same way Helena did. He pulled her back inside, noting the dull ache in his heart, that it should have been Melanie on his arm. She should see this. If they failed, perhaps she wouldn't blame him so much if she saw how formidable the enemy was. And if they failed, at least he could take comfort in the fact that Melanie had escaped the final curtain.

"Joshua, look at you!" the director said behind him.

When they turned, Josh came face to face with Director Kobyashi wearing a deep red jacket, also delicately encrusted with rhinestones. His wife, a stunning Asian-looking woman with jet black hair and flawless features, wore a matching strapless gown.

"I've been anxiously awaiting your arrival, Joshua," she said, extending to him her hand, which he kissed carefully. She wore a several carat-sized ruby on her left hand, which he avoided.

"Ping, you are as beautiful as everyone has told me you were. May I introduce Helena, who is—"

"We are acquainted, Joshua," Ping interrupted.

"Nice to see you, dear," she said, and the two women kissed each other, but Josh could feel the frostbite just as if he'd been in a blizzard.

"I was hoping our happy family would be all together and am disappointed Melanie isn't among our guests," the director barked. "Not that it isn't wonderful to see you, Helena."

His smile was brittle.

"I'm afraid there's been a little rift in our relationship, director," Josh said. "Someone else has caught her fancy. I'm hoping it's only temporary. Perhaps her newly formed and overpowering hormones."

"You should beat it out of her. Submission, Joshua, is delicious when applied equal to the indiscretion." Ping smiled and sipped her drink. Her eyes were electric, and unmistakably looking for blood.

"A lot of trouble was had to get you two together, as I'm sure you've figured out by now. It was essential to the plan. You aren't having second thoughts about helping us, are you?"

"Of course not." But he cursed himself for making a fatal flaw. He did not look the director in the eyes.

It was noted.

"May we speak in private?" Kobyashi asked.

"Absolutely, excuse me," he said to Helena.

The Director put his hand on Josh's shoulder, and

the two of them walked to the side a few paces. "A word of advice about women. They have to be told what to do, just as Ping has instructed. You'd best remember her very valuable advice."

"I realize that, sir, but—"

"Nonsense. They have to be directed. They are never to be given power to choose to walk away." He turned to watch Ping speaking with Helena and several other women. "My Ping knows if she ever tried to leave me I'd give her true death. And it wouldn't be swift. She'd pay for it."

"What are you saying?" Josh asked as she noticed several guardians surround Helena and then escort her away. He tore his eyes from the temporary distraction. "Excuse me, sir? Again?"

"No matter your feelings for Melanie, if she won't come with you, then she cannot be trusted. Unless there is something else going on?" Kobyashi's dark eyes bored into Josh's soul. He saw flames in the middle of his black orbs, with a red glow coming from somewhere deep inside him.

Joshua saw that he possessed the gift of fire.

The director looked away at the fountain. "What is it you cannot tell me, son?" he said without refocusing.

"I think she doesn't like it here. I expected her to show up tonight with another man. I think she just wanted to cause me pain."

"Which is over the line, Joshua. This should never be allowed."

"But I love her, director. Surely you understand that?"

His dark eyes danced in the red glow, and then he smiled. "No matter. We'll find you another."

Josh got the impression the director was monitoring his reaction to every one of his comments. He needed to be consistent and actually answered truthfully, "I don't want any other."

"Then she has to be re-educated. If you value her life, you will bring her in line. Wherever she's gone, she is in danger if she is not at your side, Joshua. Just remember that. If you like, I could have Ping—"

"No thank you, sir. That won't be necessary. I'll do it myself."

He'd been looking for a flaw in the man's armor, and now he had it. He didn't trust women. He trusted men perhaps only a little more.

"Can I ask you, sir, what is it that you would have me do?"

"It's all being arranged. You'll see."

Panic began to spread throughout Josh's body. He scanned the room, looking for any evidence of foul play because he felt something dangerous was about to happen. He noted several guardians holding trays, standing to attention encircling the room, watching for something that was about to happen.

The lights began to flicker as music started playing. Swimmers showed up in the pond, swimming with torches, making formations and splashing in a synchronized swimming event that was drawing praise and clapping. The entire audience was enraptured.

Josh made eye contact with Helena, who was standing with several guardians near an open doorway. Ping was not among them. The show ended in a burst of fire, as one of the torches was used to light a gas flame coming from the middle of the fountain, and then all was quiet except for the clapping.

Josh found a spotlight shone on him and the director. A microphone was handed to Kobyashi.

"Ladies and gentlemen, I give you the legendary Joshua Brandon, who has agreed to join our partnership and will be working right alongside me. Give a round of applause for him." Joshua bowed briefly, and the room cheered.

As he searched the circle of faces standing around him, he didn't see any of the house guards. All he saw were guardians. This was the time they'd talked about. But he didn't see any movement, any sudden action, or assault.

Someone was shouting off to the side, and at last, Josh's heart raced, hoping they'd started. But he was disappointed to learn the source of the interruption. Two uniformed guards held between them a woman who was struggling, who had been bloodied in some kind of skirmish. She was dressed in hiking clothes, a red cloak hung around her neck. She looked up in horror at Joshua.

Melanie!

Don't speak! She told him telepathically.

Sorely outnumbered, Josh was powerless as the director walked over to Melanie, grabbed her hair and pulled her behind him as he traversed the black floor, depositing her at Josh's feet. He stood with his legs apart, holding her up by her hair so he could see her face.

"Live or die, Joshua." Then he shouted to the room, "A test of his commitment to all of you here, let us witness the strength and passion of our partnership!"

With his other hand, Kobyashi brought out a silver jeweled knife with a blade at least seven inches long. He pointed the handle to Joshua, who began to reach for it as a weapon he wanted to dig into the director's neck, but before he could grab it, the director pulled it back, held it high, and stared down at Melanie.

"You dare to come between what we have planned

here?"

She spat at his shoes. "You can kill my immortal body, but you cannot kill my soul."

Josh readied himself to jump between them, but then he felt the burn in his hands, the familiar return of his fire. He aimed his palm at the director's head. But the flame was weak and fizzled in a limp arch, and then went out altogether.

Kobyashi laughed.

More guards arrived and grabbed Josh's arms, holding them behind him. He lunged for the knife Kobyashi held, but was unable to gain control of it.

Then they heard a blast of fire, and out from the side of the crowd stood Noel. Josh recognized the flamethrower, armed and ready to launch. Before anyone else could stop him, and while the guards were preoccupied by restraining Melanie and Joshua, before the director could muster his own fire, Noel sent out a twenty-foot arc of flame. The blaze caught Kobyashi in the chest. The director screamed, his clothes, his hair and skin on fire. Ping ran to his side where several guardians jumped on her, as others in the crowd overcame the guards easily.

The party crowd screamed and scattered through any means of escape they could find.

Josh was at last free to come to Melanie. From her

knees, she reached up to him.

He fell to her arms, clutching her close to his chest.

"How did they capture you? Did they get Jonas too?"

"No, I came back. Noel brought me back. I brought Doris' flamethrower. It was all I could think of to do."

"So stupid, Melanie. This was so stupid. You could have—"

A fresh contingency of guards showed up and were quickly tackled by several guardians, using their silver trays as shields and weapons. Josh pulled Melanie to her feet and shielded her, looking for help to get her out while he continued with the battle.

The crowd was running in confusion as a flock of blue birds began dropping little flash bombs on the audience, scattering them and sending them screaming for the entrances.

"Did you do that?" she asked him as they ran to the sides.

"Manfred's birds. And the guardians, they stood up. Everyone's going home, thank God."

He watched two guardians took Helena with them. Josh saw her try to turn her head, but they were doing what they'd been told, protect and remove her from the danger.

He picked Melanie up, unsure how hurt she was,

her blood smearing over his jacket, her head falling into his chest. He searched to the right and the left as a path was parted for him, between the smoke and the crowds. He took Melanie outside and down the steps of the red castle with the horde of others pouring from the home. He was ready to follow the crowds to the mass exodus, but he wanted to find Jonas' boys first.

He turned around, hearing someone shout his name, and saw Noel and Spencer following, trying to catch up. On his left, a long black vehicle pulled up to the entrance.

Josh didn't move.

"Go," Noel said. "They've stormed the gates at the transport station and they're all going back. Hundreds of them, Josh. Take the limo, go slip through the crowds and be free."

"You both knew about this?"

"I just got here, remember? I wasn't invited," said Spencer, as if he was being blamed for something.

"I found him, Josh," said Noel. "I brought her back on her complete, stubborn insistence. We all tried— Jonas, Audray—we all tried to talk her out of it, but she would have attempted to come on her own if I didn't accompany her. She was spotted and arrested, which was our plan so I could sneak in with this awesome device," He held up the flamethrower and grinned.

"And the guardians—they came through! So go! Leave this place and don't ever come back."

Spencer added. "But you could. You could come back and forth, just like we do."

Noel socked him in the arm.

"No, go. They'll make you director if you stay."

"But where are all his guards? His creatures I heard about?" Josh asked.

"They were burning the stables during the swim show. And the guardians passed out elixir laced with poison. Many of his guards are dead, or captured, Josh."

"Put me down!" Melanie shouted as she wiggled free.

The driver opened the door and helped Melanie into the rear seat.

"He's going to take you to the gate. Leave and don't ever come back," said Noel.

Josh ran to the dark angel and gave him a hug.

The young dark angel pushed him away with a smile. "Jonas and Audray are waiting for you up top. You can tell them all about it. They'll want to hear every detail," added Noel.

"I'll stop by sometime, and we'll go ride bikes!" Spencer said and then shrugged at the nasty look he got from Noel.

Josh sat down next to Melanie, pulled the door shut, and at last was alone with Melanie at last. She buried her head in his chest.

He could not believe their luck. Reaching down to touch her cheek, he added, "Next time, stay home. It was too—"

But she had covered his mouth with her lips, her tongue. Her hands dove into his shirt as she kissed him. "It's not going to be like that, Josh. I told you I wasn't leaving, ever. You're completely stuck with me."

Epilogue

SEVERAL HUNDRED FORMER guardians gained their freedom that day. Two of the transport stations were overrun by massive crowds. One transport vehicle was turned over and set on fire, which stopped the flow until the tracks could be cleared. Melanie and Josh were allowed to pass through the throng, literally carried above the bodies of others clamoring to get out, and then released onto the platform for a quick exit.

Other portals were guarded, manned by directorate personnel who did not know the head of the snake had been cut off. Although they no longer had any authority to report to, they held their posts until the mass exodus was complete. And then they walked away to their own freedom.

On the second day, forces inside the Underworld began to coalesce. A new leadership was quickly put into place, and order was restored and chaos was tampered down to an acceptable level. Many didn't want to leave, and once the secrets of Kobyashi and his team were revealed, there was no further support for the structure he'd set up. But the power struggle continued, as it had for centuries.

On the human side, the phenomenon of the lost persons coming back into society was difficult to explain. Not everyone returned to their families or wanted any recognition at all. Some wanted their true guardian lives restored, and many were granted, but not all. Most took advantage of the second chance for the semi-human life they'd received and deemed it lucky Joshua Brandon had negotiated such a miracle with Father. He was known as the most powerful dark angel ever to have been created. More powerful than he'd let anyone know.

Communities sprang up where these beings could exist in their dark angel form, in groups tucked away from the society at large to silently live out their immortality in relative peace. They began the work interrupted by their Underworld detour: to save human lives. As more powerful dark angels, they could fulfill their true destiny, to be of service to mankind, and to do it invisibly, without detection or recognition.

Faced with scores of choices, Joshua and Melanie retreated to the coast in Northern California in a house tucked into the hills overlooking the rugged Pacific Ocean. Surrounded by tall pines, their compound bordered a grove of old redwood trees that had been alive before any evidence of man or angel existed.

They began to fly together at sunset, as they used to do before Melanie had turned dark, appearing to the casual observer to be large cliff-dwelling birds at prey. Josh taught her how to use her body and all her powerful skills. He perfected his rebirth of fire and waited for the day he got the summons. He knew it was coming. They'd talked about their future, and until that phase of their lives was complete, nothing really could be settled. So they just lived day by day.

Noel and Spencer found themselves useful bridging the gap between the two worlds, but they attempted to keep them forever separate, as before. They also fulfilled two promises for Melanie and Josh. They returned a replacement doomsday pill to the anxious Jonas and restored to Doris, the feisty guardian and close confident of Father's, her precious flamethrower. The two dark angels found a worthy place as protectorate to Jonas' clan and others who were friends, thereby adjusting to a useful life utilizing the better sides of themselves.

They informed Josh that Helena chose to return with Annabel and had negotiated to restart her house in the old director's red home on the hill, away from the scrutiny of the human population.

Finally, Father's summons came roughly a month after Josh and Melanie had settled.

The two of them waited, watching ducks and enjoying the early morning San Francisco fog that was beginning to burn off at the Palace.

Father arrived behind them, silently, placing his hand on each of their shoulders. His voice rose above the busy work of the flock of ducks and geese that now approached, looking for food.

Melanie felt his warm fingers dig into her shoulder as if he was stabilizing his stance with her help.

"I owe you both a debt of thanks. My guardians, all of them who wanted to, are home where they belong. You should see the rejoicing going on up in Heaven. It's quite remarkable," he finished.

"I'll bet," Josh said as he turned to look at the Creator. "Has this ever happened before?"

"Never. I'm not sure it will again, either, but we'll see."

Before they could respond, he appeared in front to face the pair.

"Now that you've traveled and you've both chosen, what do you think of my little experiment?" he asked them.

"I don't feel like an experiment," she whispered back, clutching Josh's hand between them.

"No, poor choice of words, perhaps." Father rubbed his hands together, appearing to be deep in thought.

"We can't allow someone like Kobyashi to do this again," said Josh. "You have to stop letting that happen. The whole thing almost went up in smoke."

"That would be like asking these little ducklings to stop swimming. It's what they do. Dark angels and humans will take advantage as they feel like doing from time to time. But don't you think the story of what happened might lend some experience?" Father asked.

Josh shook his head. "No, someone will do it again."

"Then I suppose it can't be stopped."

Melanie sat up straighter. "Why don't you stop it? You could, couldn't you?"

"Not sure I want to. What better lesson? How will my creations grow if they can't be trusted to make mistakes? You think my lack of interference means I don't care? On the contrary, the story continues. Imperfect. As it should be."

"But all the pain and suffering. It just seems so unnecessary," she returned. She didn't understand his position. "If you can stop it, why would you allow people to have to go through all this chaos?"

"Because look at what it did to Joshua. You called

the human world vanilla, remember?"

"Guilty as charged."

"Life doesn't exist, although you're in a better situation to do that than most. Life is earned, isn't it? Melanie, your father taught you how to ride a bicycle, use your skates, ride a horse? It's no different. Everyone falls, picks themselves up, and then makes a decision. The Underworld serves that function. People will keep making bad decisions until they make good ones. Like life, free will is what happens, while they're making other plans, as was so famously said."

She began to understand why Claire had loved Father so much. She envied her friend's years of friendship and inspiration.

"All of that is available to you too, my child. But you have to choose. What is it the both of you desire?"

Josh turned to look into her eyes. "You choose."

"What are my choices?" she asked, suddenly afraid to speak.

Father shrugged. "You try the experiment. If you were in my position, what would you grant?"

"You mean like a favor? You're giving us the chance at a favor?"

"Within reason, whatever that is," he chuckled.

She stretched out her arms. "I love this body. I love being powerful. I have so much I want to do. I want to live forever." She examined her lover's face. "I want to be with Joshua for eternity. But…"

"She's worried that as a dark angel she will not be able to have children. She wants children," Josh explained.

"No, that's not right. I want your children, Josh. I want our children. And that's not possible, right?"

"Is that what you want? You want to outlive your children? They would be born mortal."

"Why can't they be born immortal? Why can't we have that?"

"You mean immortal, set in stone, but at what age? You want them to grow, to learn, to develop? Or do you want children created from each of you that stay the same forever, like you two will?"

"Melanie, it means do you want to be powerful, or do you want to be a human mother, like Claire, like Audray. That's the choice for you."

"And for you."

"No, it's your choice."

"And I can't have both?" she asked.

"No, my child, that's not possible. You can't be two people at the same time, can you? It goes to what you really want."

Melanie didn't want to make the choice. She didn't feel qualified to do so. It was so unfair, all these decisions and changes that had happened in such a short period of time. Then she began to giggle.

"What is it?" Josh asked.

"I choose not to decide. I choose to decide later. If I come to you, Father, and ask to change my mind, will this choice still be available to me?"

"I don't see why not."

"Is that being fair to you?" she asked the man she wanted to spend the rest of her days with. They would be long days, short days, whatever. But they would be together. His answer came in the form of a smile, a nod, and a kiss.

"So you see? We can have it both ways, Father. You were wrong."

The old man laughed. "Child, I'm wrong all the time. I make more mistakes than you can ever imagine. Come." He held his arms out to the sides, hugging them both.

AT HOME, THE glow of the fireplace light on his face softened his features. He whispered, "I think you chose wisely for us. We'll know, Melanie, when it's time."

She chuckled at her silly thoughts. "Who would ever believe me if I said we had the choice to live forever or become human? I guess I couldn't choose because I didn't want to give up the forever with you."

"I will promise to make it the very best it can be, my love."

Did you enjoy Redemption? If you enjoyed this world of angels, guardian angels and dark angels, why not try Gideon's story, the half-angel half-vampire being created by mistake? You can order a copy for yourself here.

authorsharonhamilton.com/portfolio-item/gideon

Here's an excerpt from the first chapter of the book, Gideon, Fall From Grace, Book 1:

THE MONSTROUS PURPLE bus barreled down Highway 101 at eighty miles an hour. Multicolored block letters were shrink-wrapped onto the hulking frame: Blood Bank of the Redwoods. Gideon was still shocked it had been so easy to steal the beast. Flapped his wings and showed his fangs, and the technician was out of there.

Motivating the decision today to take his life into his own hands, he was completely done with being isolated, separated from all the other Guardians called to missions by "Father" in his infinite wisdom. *Father* was not nearly the right name to describe the heartless codger he labeled Supreme Being, or SB. The only mission given to Gideon was to watch and report. Be a spy on the civilian population.

A Watcher wasn't a doer.

Like all the other Watchers before him, his job was to help the Guardians save lives, and by saving lives they saved souls.

He'd seen thousands of them carting the civilians' precious cargo, their red elixir of life. Gideon had always wanted to drive one. Today had been a true Red Letter Day, the best day of his life so far. Coming over the Marin grade, the stainless-steel beast almost leapt off the pavement like a skateboard as the freeway suddenly made a steep dip, heading toward San Francisco.

Happy to be down off his perch atop the North Tower of the Golden Gate Bridge where he had spent the last fifty years of his immortal life, Gideon was finally looking forward to a future carved by his own hand. Probably a dark one. When earlier today he'd used his wings, searching for the bus in Marin, they were white, as all Guardians' wings were, but he suspected by sunset they'd turn black.

Worst, coldest fuckin' job in the universe. Did the Supreme Being hate him that much? And what had he ever done to deserve this? Could he help it if he saw the human population as flesh sacs? That's what they were. He was tired of pretending, holding back his true vampiric nature. He had to stuff down his urges so he wouldn't become a piece of scorched meat buried in Heaven's graveyard somewhere. None of it was easy, with the incessant singing and Guardianship classes in gardening and lacemaking, which nearly drove him insane. Maybe he was insane. A person *would have to be* insane to be *that* happy and cheerful all the time.

Fuck that shit.

He was bored to death. It took a saint to endure that kind of life. He'd even begun to bring heavy weapons to work with him like he was looking for a large enough target to use them on. He had fantasies about taking down a blimp or a cargo ship.

I'm an angel messenger all right. I'm going postal.

Being stuck there was worse than being ignored. He was buried. Buried alive in the human world on top of the coldest fuckin' bridge in the state, the only heat coming from the glow and meager warmth of the red lamp sitting beneath his butt on his perch atop the massive metal structure. The Supreme Being was cruel, and contrary to what the Guardians preached to him, SB did not know the meaning of the word compassion. Or pleasure. Or ecstasy.

Why leave him up there alone to suffer? He knew the asshole was watching, could feel His eyes on his back. Probably the kind of guy who liked to pick the wings off flies and watch them run around chained by gravity. Tasking Gideon an eternity to make calls to Guardians so they could swoop down in their gossamer-winged finery and save humans from jumping? And be okay with letting them get all the credit for the "saves"? The celebrations of their victories were the worst. Cherub choirs hurt his ears with their incessant clapping and yodeling in preternatural form humans couldn't hear.

No, the Golden Gate Bridge might be a little better than Heaven. But just a little.

Harkening back to his old vampiric nature, he'd taken to counting again. It was what he did when he was nervous or when things weren't going his way. He'd count ships that passed underneath. Count the cruise ships to Alcatraz. Count the freighters, the rice rocket cargo ships, and the dirty tankers. He even counted the number of cargo containers and grouped them into types by color, size, and branding. Occasionally, he'd get to count a pleasure yacht or sailing ship. What was he supposed to do? Pray? What a useless waste of time.

Sometimes he'd go days without a jumper. Others, there could be a handful. They seemed to run in bunches, like grapes. Perhaps it was the pattern of the "circle of life" in the human world. Or the Pacific Ocean's currents or winds. Perhaps the pull of the moon or pollution or traffic. Who knew?

Let 'em jump. If they want to die, let them rest in peace. Float a target out there so they can hit the bull's eye—go out with a perfect score, so to speak.

And then there'd be one asshole who'd miss and spend his last remaining seconds feeling a complete failure. He hated sharing their angst, something he was fully privy to. The fear was one thing he could tolerate, but their regrets, who needed it? He had enough of his own, enough for the whole human race and half the vampire race as well.

No, going out, missing the imaginary target and scoring a fuckin' zero was the way to go. They were losers anyway. Might as well claim that last desperate act as a loser.

He was living proof not everyone wanted to be saved. He'd always thought vampires would wind up in the Underworld. But no, that wasn't the way of Heaven, and it wasn't his destiny. Just as not all the jumpers were saved, not every vampire wound up down below. What made him so special, he wondered. So what if a bunch of the human population and a few vamps wanted to end themselves?

No, Gideon thought, redemption was a dirty word and highly overrated.

He'd seen the Guardians' super sanctimonious smiles while they fluttered back up to Heaven in a shower of golden sparkles. He'd seen them arrive home to a cheering crowd of angelic hoards and cherub choirs that hurt Gideon's sensitive ears. And never once did any of them stop and bother to say thank you to him. Not once.

What's up with that?

Maybe they knew about his bloodlust. He knew SB understood, but he wasn't sure about the Guardians. It had been one colossal fuckup, turning him into an angel. He wasn't capable of dying anyway, and he probably wouldn't have even if some damned Guardian hadn't decided to show mercy on him. The little do-gooder thought his wounds were life-threatening, that he'd been trying to save the young lady when he was actually going to drain her after he'd pushed her out of the way of the truck that clipped him. Miss-Goody-Two-Shoes fucked up his whole life. He'd been swooped up, fitted with wings he never wanted—he already could fly—"saved" they called it. More like fucked. And not in the way he liked, either. This was the fucking kind of fucked where the fuckee didn't leave with a smile on his face.

His days in Heaven were tortured with music, which gave him migraines. The sunlight burned his eyes. How he'd like to drain the lifeblood from all their chubby cheeks.

He thought about the nubile young Guardians, especially the redheads, turned in their prime. Their lusciously smooth bodies definitely had heavenly curves. He lived in a state of stiff arousal those long years of his angel training classes, in such close proximity to such lovely, naïve creatures. His sensitive skin craved to touch them as his fangs yearned to plunge deep and coat his throat with their sweet lifeblood. His ears had buzzed and his nose itched 24/7.

Their scent was addicting. It would only be a matter of time before the warnings and spells would no longer work on him, and he'd do his share of rutting through the entire redhead population. And that would never do. But it might have earned him a ticket down below. He was counting on that today. He wanted out of a life he never chose, but hoped he could alter.

So he was going to leave in a blaze of glory. Catch the attention of the Guardians who had ignored him for so long. Steal a Blood Bank bus, suck out the entire inventory, and send it over the edge. Go commiserate with his buddies down below where he heard the action was much better and the climate more to his liking.

Supreme Fucktard must have known he'd have a breaking point. So maybe that's why they'd sent him up to the top of the North Tower. At first, he was relieved to be away from the choirs and angel dust, standing up above the fog line like he was in charge of the whole bay. But, as the years went by, it got worse and worse.

Even though they gave him an estate in Sonoma County where he could play around with winemaking on his one day off, he was utterly and completely bored. Making wine wasn't at all like what he remembered of making love. He should have used his estate as a love nest. Perhaps they would have overlooked his indiscretion, violating the directive never to bed a female of any sort as long as he remained angel.

Well bugger that.

Practically no one ever visited him except his angel friend, Francis, the ex-Priest who took his Sunday shift. All his other friends had screwed up and been spirited away to the Underworld years ago. Francis just had to make sure he didn't get too drunk and fall off that North Tower. That would surprise a commuter. A drunken Guardian on the windshield on the way to work? That was actually something he'd *like* to watch. Francis's old angry Russian friend had nearly done that once.

Gideon spent his other six days counting whatever passed by him or through the straights, even seagulls. He knew how many houseboats and boats were anchored in Sausalito on any given day. He'd count cars, then just red cars, cars with ski racks, cars with barking dogs, cars with women who hiked up their skirts so high he could see all those private parts eternally denied him.

So maybe SB had a plan. If he did, Gideon would be the last to know, that was for sure.

Does he even freakin' know how freakin' cold it was up there?

The purple beast veered when the freeway took a sharp turn to the left. The sloppy box-like manufacture of the vehicle was becoming more difficult to control the faster he went. Sticky dark red blood was leaking from the crack at the base of the enormous mobile Blood Bank's rear doors. Gideon had been tossing back empty bags of plasma after he'd torn off the tops and drained them. After fifty years, the blood still made him hard. Harder than one of those fucking towers, and just as tall too.

Definitely going to have to do something about that. He'd be in some real pain in an hour.

He finished a bag and tossed it through the blown-out driver's side window. He watched through the side mirror as the long red finger of blood swirled in the air behind him until it landed on someone's windshield.

To a motorist from behind, it would look like the doors themselves were leaking. The blood began as droplets, but soon cascaded in ribbons and flew in the breeze like little red snippets of flags as the bus swerved.

Hard to peer through blood-soaked wipers when you're going at sixty-plus miles per hour, he thought, as he saw drivers behind him deal with the visibility issue, probably thinking they'd hit a bird or some other animal. Scanning his side mirror again, he spotted a vehicle pileup several hundred yards behind him, amidst smoke and steam. It managed to block a California Highway Patrolman. His red light flashed impotently behind the mound of cars acting as a barrier, while Gideon's bus sped along to relative safety, if that's what it could be called.

To infinity and beyond.

Gideon smiled. This was turning out to be a nice day, after all. Causing havoc lightened his mood. Being invisible for so long actually made him giddy to create such a splash. And how the news media would play this one up. Yeah, it was going to be fun watching all that.

He was going to get a motel room in the city, eat In-N-Out burgers and those thick chocolate shakes, watch porno, and pretend some little hottie was going to screw him senseless. Maybe the little unlucky redhead at the back of the bus would survive the ordeal.

He flashed a cool grin and enjoyed the air whistling in from the vacant windshield he'd kicked out. The ocean breeze tangled with his straggly dirty blond hair, struggling to stay in the ponytail he'd fastened.

Joy. He realized he actually began to understand what the Guardians called joy.

They didn't have a decent sound system on the purple beast, but it did have an aging CD player mounted and swinging back and forth. It was attached with a red and yellow striped bungee cord wrapped around the oversized rearview mirror stem. Somebody probably had to bring their own music to calm the faint of heart as they drew out that wonderful red honey. Keep the customers calm. Get them to give it up for free like that girl at the prom some seventy years ago.

Now that was a nice night.

He grabbed for another bag in the egg crate at his feet, roared as he felt his fangs come back to life—longer, whiter, and sharper. He sucked the elixir and then swore as his dick elongated another inch, pushing against the steering wheel, causing the bus to swerve and almost topple. He adjusted himself and continued to drive with new focus.

Not yet. Can't crash yet.

It had been an impulse decision to steal the bus. With his man toys of destruction strapped to his back, he'd been cruising overhead, excited about leaving his perch on the bridge, and all of a sudden it was like the Heavens opened. The purple bus was right there below him, ripe and ready for its voyage into the unknown.

He'd barked at the male tech who was gassing up the vehicle and then fled on foot, without Gideon having to lay a finger on him. They didn't have any decent music. Only thing he could find were *Phantom of the Opera* CDs stashed in a hole in the dashboard. He left the little redheaded phlebotomist hiding in the back as he fired up the engine and streaked off towards San Francisco, the gas line still briefly attached. No need for a fill-up today.

Today, we're going to fly.

He could hear her frantically whispering on her cell phone from the bathroom, as if the cardboard walls of the bus would shield her calls for help.

"I agreed to one date. You said the guy was nice. Well, he's gone now this monster has taken the bus.

I'm stuck in the back," she was saying. "Don't think he knows I'm here. Please, send someone. I didn't sign up for this."

Gideon smiled. His dick lurched so he slapped it down with another growl. He'd unwittingly found a *professional*. Talk about his lucky day! If she survived, perhaps she could be an evening snack, and God knew he liked to play with his food first. He hadn't had a bite of that for over fifty years. Christ, he'd practically been a priest.

The *Phantom* CD was at max.

"I'll be beside you. To comfort and to guide you."

He had a lot in common with the Phantom, he thought, as he entered the Rainbow Tunnel just north of the bridge. He howled through the open windows and heard the echo of his own voice bounce off the arched tube. It would scare everyone inside the structure, but it made his soul turn to flame. He gained on a family in a green Jeep to his right, the dad giving him the once over, not sure what he was really seeing. The driver slowed down and let Gideon pass.

"Smart fellow," Gideon mumbled.

Coming upon the bridge approach, he saw the silver and white skyline of the City, contrasted with the deep blue Pacific Ocean on both sides, dotted with little white sailboats on the Bay side. He swerved to the slow lane. It was such a clear, sunny morning, well before the fog rolled in. His heart raced, thrilled to capacity, as his face and hands began to glow.

"Careful, little one," he called out to a well-muscled woman in her early thirties, dressed in pink, bicycling toward the City. He watched her perfect form, her shapely body, her heart-shaped ass, and decided not to sideswipe her. Some people were just too beautiful to waste. Remembering his mission, he punched down on the pedal, sending a billow of gray smoke out the back as the bus lurched and picked up speed.

He reached down to the floor and pulled up his Carl Gustav 84 mm rocket launcher. One-handed, he aimed it out through the busted windshield, towards the thick cable equidistant between the two towers, the blue open mouth of the bay visible beyond. Holding the tripod of the loaded weapon along his thigh, he pulled the trigger. It hurt like a son of a bitch. He hadn't been too careful; its vibration took out the strip of metal that used to separate the two windshields. But no matter. The anti-tank projectile preceded his forward movement, hitting the bridge cable dead center, snapping it a few seconds before the bus got there. It also took out a twenty-foot section of railing and part of the roadway. Support cables instantly coiled and waved in the air like snakes after being sprung. One tiny adjustment of the steering wheel to the right, and the monstrous purple bus headed off the bridge through the gaping hole, on its maiden flight.

He wondered if this was how it felt to be in a dirigible, wafting through thin air with only the sound of the wind whistling through the window holes.

Time stood still. He saw the cup glued to the dash filled with shuddering pencils, so he tossed them out the driver's side and watched as they found their own way. He wondered what it would look like, his big purple bus and the pencils and blood flying in the air in free fall. He searched for other objects that might impale him and found none. He wondered if there were any Guardians out there yet, if there would be angelic witnesses to this historic flight. He couldn't wait to hear the rumors.

Except now he would join the ranks of the fallen—a casualty of trying to be so good for way too long.

SB really should have known better. It's not nice to fool Mother Nature.

Purchase Gideon, Fall From Grace, here.
authorsharonhamilton.com/portfolio-item/gideon

Or, if you want more paranormal romance, have you tried the Golden Vampires of Tuscany series, starting with Book 1, Honeymoon Bite? This series of four books is just waiting for you to explore more of Sharon's twisted sister, S. Hamil.

And there are more planned. Stay tuned, and sign up for my Newsletter so you don't miss an ounce of news!

About the Author

S. HAMIL, Sharon Hamilton's twisted sister, writes paranormal romance with a central theme of the healing power of true love. Her characters from multiple worlds including Heaven and the Underworld are angels, dark angels, vampires and some who are not quite sure what they are. They follow a bumpy path to redemption, but not exactly what they taught you in Sunday School!

She loves hearing from her fans:
Sharonhamilton2001@gmail.com

Her website is:
sharonhamiltonauthor.com

Find out more about S. Hamil, her upcoming releases, appearances and news when you sign up for S. Hamil's newsletter.

Facebook:
facebook.com/SharonHamiltonAuthor

Twitter:
twitter.com/sharonlhamilton

Pinterest:
pinterest.com/AuthorSharonH

Amazon:
amazon.com/Sharon-Hamilton/e/B004FQQMAC

BookBub:
bookbub.com/authors/sharon-hamilton

Youtube:
youtube.com/channel/UCDInkxXFpXp_4Vnq08ZxMBQ

Soundcloud:
soundcloud.com/sharon-hamilton-1

S. Hamil's Rockin' Romance Readers:
facebook.com/groups/sealteamromance

S. Hamil's Goodreads Group:
goodreads.com/group/show/199125-sharon-hamilton-readers-group

Visit S. Hamil's Online Store:
sharon-hamilton-author.myshopify.com

Join S. Hamil's Review Teams:

eBook Reviews:
sharonhamiltonassistant@gmail.com

Audio Reviews:
sharonhamiltonassistant@gmail.com

__Life__ is one fool thing after another.
__Love__ is two fool things after each other.

Reviews

had me anticipating what would happen next many times over, so much so I could not put it down and even finished it up in a day. The vampires in this book were different from your average vampire, but I enjoy different variations and changes to the same old stuff. It made for a more unpredictable read and more adventurous to explore! Vampire lovers, any paranormal readers and even those who love the romance genre will enjoy Honeymoon Bite."

"This is the first non-Seal book of this author's I have read and I loved it. There is a cast-like hierarchy in this vampire community with humans at the very bottom and Golden vampires at the top. Lionel is a dark vampire who are servants of the Goldens. Phoebe is a Golden who has not decided if she will remain human or accept the turning to become a vampire. Either way she and Lionel can never be together since it is forbidden.

I enjoyed this story and I am looking forward to the next installment."

"A hauntingly romantic read. Old love lost and new love found. Family, heart, intrigue and vampires. Grabbed my attention and couldn't put down. Would definitely recommend."

PRAISE FOR THE
SEAL BROTHERHOOD SERIES

"Fans of Navy SEAL romance, I found a new author to feed your addiction. Finely written and loaded delicious with moments, Sharon Hamilton's storytelling satisfies like a thick bar of chocolate." —Marliss Melton, bestselling author of the *Team Twelve* Navy SEALs series

"Sharon Hamilton does an EXCELLENT job of fitting all the characters into a brotherhood of SEALS that may not be real but sure makes you feel that you have entered the circle and security of their world. The stories intertwine with each book before...and each book after and THAT is what makes Sharon Hamilton's SEAL Brotherhood Series so very interesting. You won't want to put down ANY of her books and they will keep you reading into the night when you should be sleeping. Start with this book...and you will not want to stop until you've read the whole series and then...you will be waiting for Sharon to write the next one." (5 Star Review)

"Kyle and Christy explode all over the pages in this first book, *[Accidental SEAL]*, in a whole new series of SEALs. If the twist and turns don't get your heart jumping, then maybe the suspense will. This is a must read for those that are looking for love and adventure with a little sloppy love thrown in for good measure." (5 Star Review)

PRAISE FOR THE
BAD BOYS OF SEAL TEAM 3 SERIES

"I love reading this series! Once you start these books, you can hardly put them down. The mix of romance and suspense keeps you turning the pages one right after another! Can't wait until the next book!" (5 Star Review)

"I love all of Sharon's Seal books, but *[SEAL's Code]* may just be her best to date. Danny and Luci's journey is filled with a wonderful insight into the Native American life. It is a love story that will fill you with warmth and contentment. You will enjoy Danny's journey to become a SEAL and his reasons for it. Good job Sharon!" (5 Star Review)

PRAISE FOR THE
BAND OF BACHELORS SERIES

"[Lucas] was the first book in the Band of Bachelors series and it was a phenomenal start. I loved how we got to see the other SEALs we all love and we got a look at Lucas and Marcy. They had an instant attraction, and their love was very intense. This book had it all, suspense, steamy romance, humor, everything you want in a riveting, outstanding read. I can't wait to read the next book in this series." (5 Star Review)

PRAISE FOR THE
TRUE BLUE SEALS SERIES

"Keep the tissues box nearby as you read *True Blue SEALs: Zak* by Sharon Hamilton. I imagine more than I wish to that the circumstances surrounding Zak and Amy are all too real for returning military personnel and their families. Ms. Hamilton has put us right in the middle of struggles and successes that these two high school sweethearts endure. I have read several of Sharon Hamilton's military romances but will say this is the most emotionally intense of the ones that I have read. This is a well-written, realistic story with authentic characters that will have you rooting for them and proud of those who serve to keep us safe. This is an author who writes amazing stories that you love and cry with the characters. Fans of Jessica Scott and Marliss Melton will want to add Sharon Hamilton to their list of realistic military romance writers." (5 Star Review)